To Karen
with much love
Shirley Oliver
x

Together Forever Apart

S.E. OLIVER

authorHOUSE®

AuthorHouse™ UK
1663 Liberty Drive
Bloomington, IN 47403 USA
www.authorhouse.co.uk
Phone: 0800 047 8203 (Domestic TFN)
+44 1908 723714 (International)

Published by AuthorHouse 02/03/2020

ISBN: 978-1-7283-9836-5 (sc)
ISBN: 978-1-7283-9835-8 (e)

Dedicated to Victor and Nora. For the good times.

Chapter One

"I'm sorry Nikki but I don't think we should see each other anymore" he said, continuing to stare straight ahead and making no attempt to look at her. Nikki felt a pain go through her so intense she could hardly breathe. They hadn't come this far to throw it all away now. But rather than get angry, she calmly sat down and took a sip of coffee.

"Did you hear me?" asked Pip. "Leave Nik, just leave."

From where she was sitting she could see a tear roll down his cheek.

"I heard you," she replied gently. "And if I thought you really meant it, I go. But you don't. I know you too well. Something's wrong and you just want to protect me from it. But darling, I'm not going anywhere. I promised you years ago I'd always be yours. Just because we didn't actually say any marriage vows, well not to each other anyway, I meant to love you forever, through the good times and the bad. Whatever's happened Pip, nothing will change the way I feel about you. Please let me help you." Nikki took another sip of coffee before adding, "you can start by telling me the truth about the stabbing".

"Bugger you can nag," said Pip as he sat down beside her. A slight smile came across his face.

"It's a real mess Nik, and I don't want to involve you. To be honest I feel as if my head's going to burst with all that's going on. And having an affair is the last thing I need right now".

Nikki glared at him.

"Well stop thinking of us as an affair then, we are so much more than that and you know it. I thought I was your best friend? And confidante too?" she said firmly.

"Fair play," smiled Pip, "as long as your don't try and seduce me while you're being my friend. I don't think I could manage anything else at the moment!"

This was more like <u>her</u> Pip.

The one she had fallen in love with all those years earlier...

At the age of twelve, trips to the local hospital three times a week for physiotherapy were, to say the least, tedious. Nikki and her mother had been making visits for more than two years now. Marion Edwards was wonderful. She never once complained, even though it had meant putting her life on hold somewhat to support her daughter through her painful treatment. Every Monday, Wednesday and Friday afternoon the two of them would take the twenty five minute bus ride that quite literally went all round the houses, to travel what would otherwise have been a short distance to the hospitals outpatient department.

Often as a distraction, Marion would point out the wonders of nature's ever changing colours in the various trees that lined their route. And this was to continue each season, every season for nearly eight years.

The surgery on Nikki's legs had been difficult and annoyingly regular in her young life. Complications had resulted in her being in a wheelchair or on crutches for most of her teenage years. But she was a fighter. She kept cheerful and was more than a little determined that one day she would be able to walk well again. No-one would know of the suffering she had endured, unless she chose to tell them.

Marion sat in her usual seat in the reception area whilst her daughter underwent her treatment. She would pass the time knitting bonnets and tiny cardigans for the babies in the premature baby unit, or blanket squares for the elderly in the nursing home or some other deserving cause that had displayed a request on the rather messy notice board. She was well known to the nursing staff and had made it her business to welcome new patients. Marion was the most caring and unselfish women you could meet. She genuinely cared for others and gave the precious gift of her own time to those who needed it. This often meant that they would be an extra half an hour or so leaving if Marion was deep in conversation with someone grateful of her sympathetic ear. Nikki sometimes found this frustrating, especially if her physio session had been particularly distressing. Some of the treatments involved Nikki's legs being packed in ice. This was supposed to make the manipulation of the muscles easier and cause less pain, but she was never convinced it did. She did however want to get home before she thawed out!

In September of 1974 Nikki started senior school. The school building was old and not at all disability friendly. To be honest, back then, anyone who needed additional care was either sent somewhere other than main stream school or tutored at home. It was only because she had an elder sister at the school that she was even considered a place. The teaching staff at Nikki's school were amazing and went out of their way to ensure she could attend as much as possible. She was a popular girl with both the teachers and her peers and their support kept her both cheerful and positive. Obviously, the amount of time she spent in hospital affected her school work but she was a bright girl, eager to learn and made every effort to catch up as much as she could. Her mother was an 'Old County High' gal, well educated and extremely well read. She had become a secretary after leaving school for a publishing company and had continued to work part time, for the same employer after having Suzanne and Nikki. This was by no means a chore. It enabled her to keep up to date with the latest publications but better still, gave her unlimited access to books of all interests and genre. This in turn, was of great benefit to Nikki as she and her mother would spend hours reading poetry and short stories as well as factual books on history and science. Marion was horrified that schools had apparently ceased to teach *proper* history, as she put it. How could you possibly get through life not learning by heart the full and comprehensive list of the Kings and Queens of England, births, deaths and reigns? Unthinkable! So in addition to the school taught modern history, Nikki was taught the more relevant stuff, or so it was considered by her mother. The same applied to geography, "How the re-development of the local shopping precinct is ever going to help you travel through Europe, is beyond me," was one of Marions more popular phrases. French lessons passed Nikki by completely. She missed at least two double lessons a week due to hospital appointments. When the time came to take her French 'O' level, Madame Dubois insisted she should sit the paper. 'You will get a mark just for writing your name at the top of the page,' she said. Nikki didn't want to fail with only one mark, so on the day of the exam, she stayed away.

Wednesday's physiotherapy appointment was much the same as any other. Nikki came out of the cubicle with her leg cold and numb from being packed in ice. She was in pain and relieved the session was over. She just wanted to go home. Her mother looked up and smiled at her.

"How did it go?" she asked, saddened by her daughter's obvious discomfort. "Sit down sweetheart," she continued. "I just want to finish this little bonnet then I can leave it at reception on the way out for the baby unit." Nikki sat down and waited. Just as they were about to leave, a tall, dark haired man, of about thirty approached them.

"Hello, do you mind if I join you for a while, I won't keep you long, I can see you've had enough for one day." He smiled at Nikki. Mrs Edwards shuffled up to make room for him. "My name's Philip Scrarrow, everyone calls me Pip. I'm a volunteer with a scheme that tries to help young people, like yourself, get back to enjoying a normal life. We offer outings and residential trips that encourage rehabilitation through sport, hobbies, workshops and challenges. It's a lot more fun than just exercises here."

Marion looked interested and started to ask lots of questions.

"Please don't think me rude," said Pip, "but I need to hear what Nikki thinks. It _is_ about her after all." Nikki began to feel rather special. He turned to Nikki and smiled at her again and as he did Nikki felt something she had never experienced in her young life before. Isn't it funny, when you feel like that? She was convinced everyone could see how she felt. They don't of course, but you think they do. How could they not? The feeling must be visible on the outside, as it was so intense on the inside. You feel so different, you must look different too. How could someone you've only just met have such an effect on you? And just what was it she felt exactly? Flustered? Excited? Awkward? All of these things and more. A rush of emotions the likes of which she'd never known. He was lovely. Not jaw droppingly handsome but a good looking man, with a strong, fit body. He had a gentle tone in his voice, caring and kind in the way he spoke. He was without doubt, the most wonderful man Nikki had ever met.

Pip explained that the next camp was to be in Norfolk at the end of May and if Nikki would like to be part of it, they could let him know at next week's visit. He handed them some literature to take away with them. He shook Mrs Edwards hand and turned to Nikki.

"I really hope you will be able to come," he said. "You'll have a great time, I promise." Nikki feel a wave sweep over her with such a force she thought she might faint.

Mrs Edwards sat next to Nikki on the bus on the way home chatting about the trip. She wasn't convinced it would be the right thing for her daughter to do. She was worried she may hurt herself further and wasn't prepared to make a decision before discussing it with Nikki's father. Nikki wasn't really listening, she was thinking about Pip. Obviously this is what was meant by a school girl crush. Instant, intense and quite overwhelming but a crush nevertheless, nothing more, how could it be? She was only twelve for heaven's sake and he was much older. Much, much older.

After showing her father the leaflet, they agreed that as long as she promised to be careful the trip may be just the thing to help Nikki recover. Nikki was so excited. For the first time she couldn't wait for the next ice packed session at the hospital but only because she knew she would see Pip and be able to tell him she could go on the trip. As the appointment approached, she felt sick with excitement at the thought of seeing him again. She hadn't told anyone about him, or how she felt. Her sister Suzanne, would have just called her stupid and friends would just have thought him far too old. She didn't want to hear either of these opinions, so she kept him to herself.

As Nikki came out of the 'torture chamber', (as Christine, the physiotherapist liked to refer to it, which seemed to amuse her) she saw a young woman talking to her mother. Nikki plonked herself down next to her in most ungainly way. If was difficult to do much else as she could hardly bend her knees. She expected her to be another patient. She wasn't.

"This is Sally," said Marion, "she's from the 'Bright Future' scheme and has come to collect your details for the trip in May."

Nikki's heart sank. Where was Pip? She had been so looking forward to seeing him today. Sally was really nice and Nikki warmed to her as they talked in more detail about the trip. She became more excited about the adventure despite being sad not to have seen Pip.

Two weeks before Nikki was due to leave for Norfolk, she developed a problem with her knee which required immediate surgery. Devastated, she was re-admitted to hospital and consequently missed the trip.

She wasn't to see Pip again for another four years.

Chapter Two

Missing out on the trip was a shame and Nikki didn't get another chance. However, she was encouraged by others at the hospital, to be a little braver and soon gained the confidence to start going out and about a bit more. Since the surgery had started, her life had been a constant circle of hospital, school, home, hospital, more of the same and not much else. She needed to socialize more, meet new people and start living a normal teenage life. The local youth club was held in the church hall, less than half a mile from her home. One Friday evening, Nikki, her sister Suzanne and school friend Lyn decided to give it a try. It was quite good, as youth clubs go. Suzanne was two years older than Nikki. She was taller by a good three inches. Her long brown hair and brown eyes were a sharp contrast to her younger sisters who had always kept her blonde hair short and messy. Suzanne was also slender and really quite elegant, where as Nikki had very defined and developed muscles due to the amount of physiotherapy. Despite the physical differences it was obvious they were sisters and they always looked out for each other.

There were around forty young people at the club. Some of the lads had formed a band. This consisted of an excellent lead guitarist (who pretty much carried the others) a drummer, bassist, rhythm guitarist, second percussionist and a singer who tended to shout far more than he sang. But they amused the rest of the club members, which was just as well as there was no chance of getting away from the noise they made. After a few tuneless months they began to get quite good and even got a few bookings. The band went under the name of 'Desdin'. This had been given to them by one of the youth workers. The lead guitarists name was Des and the band made a din! However, the leader had convinced them it was a clever name as they were destined for better things. Nikki liked the club and the second week a leader by the name of Steve came over to introduce himself.

"Hi," he shouted as he tried to be heard over Desdin's latest attempt of Status Quo's 'Paper Plane'. "I saw you last week but you left early and I never got the chance to introduce myself."

"I'm Nikki," shouted Nikki. "And this is my friend Lyn, sorry I didn't catch your name?"

"I'm Steve," he bellowed just as the band stopped playing. Everyone laughed.

"Hi," came a chorus of twenty or so voices. Steve roared with laughter and Nikki instantly liked him. They chatted and he asked her about her need for crutches.

"Broke your leg?"

"Bit more complicated than that," replied Nikki. She was happy to tell Steve and frankly was quite relieved he'd asked her. So many people avoided asking Nikki directly in an attempt to avoid upsetting her. Sometimes this had the complete opposite effect. She recalled one occasion she was in her wheel chair, being pushed along by her mother. A woman stopped to talk to her. 'How is she?' she had asked Mrs Edwards, whispering over the top of Nikki's head.

"It's my <u>legs</u> not my hearing I'm having a problem with," said Nikki. Marion apologised to the woman for Nikki's rudeness. "People don't understand," said Marion.

"Well they never will if every time they see someone in a chair, they treat them like a moron!" retorted Nikki. "There's nothing wrong with me other than the fact I have painful legs, doesn't mean I've stopped having feelings. Stupid cow."

"That's enough Nicola," snapped Marion. Nikki knew it was best to shut up when she was addressed by her full name; she didn't what to upset her mum. It was stressful for her too.

Steve was interested and although he showed genuine compassion, was not in the slightest way patronising. He seemed to understand how she felt and more importantly, how she wanted to be treated.

"Just going to get some crisps and coke," he said. "What can I get you two?"

"We can get our own, she's not a cripple," said Lyn.

"Shut up Lyn, he didn't say I was," said Nikki. Lyn went off to get her own while Steve picked up the drinks and two packets of ready salted for him & Nikki. As ten o'clock approached, Steve was at the door to say goodnight to everyone. He was handing out slips of paper to remind them all of the barbeque next Friday evening, to be held in the woods on the outskirts of town.

"You will come Nikki, won't you?" asked Steve.

"I don't know if I can," she replied, "I'm not very good

on uneven surfaces and I don't know how I'd get there either."

"Well we must do something about that," said Steve "It'll be great fun, we can't have you missing out. Leave it with me."

Nikki smiled. "Thank you," she said feeling a little apprehensive but flattered by the attention.

"He fancies you," said Lyn as they made they made their way home.

"Don't be so silly," said Nikki. "He's just trying to include me, that's all. It's nice. I wish more people were more like him."

"What's that 'sposed to mean?" snorted Lyn.

"I didn't mean you, it's just some people can be unkind, Steve isn't, that's all," said Nikki.

"You fancy him too, don't you?" giggled Lyn.

Nikki smiled. "I like him, he's nice."

"He's old Nik, he must be at least twenty."

"Oh do grow up Lyn, we're going on a youth club barbeque, not getting married."

"Ah, so you do fancy him if you thinking about getting married," teased Lyn.

"Maybe," giggled Nikki.

Steve was twenty-two when he and Nikki started going out together, Nikki was three months off her fifteenth birthday. He was great fun, supportive and helped Nikki through a lot of her treatments. Her parents liked him and thought he was kind to help Nikki as much as he did. Nikki wasn't so sure they would have been quite so keen on him if they had realized the intensity of their relationship. Nikki and Steve grew very close. He was at university and being away from home was glad of the kind hospitality shown to him by Nikki's parents in the form of home cooked meals. Mr Edwards would, on occasions, lend Steve the family car to enable him to take Nikki on an outing.

As people get older, age differences between couples matters less and less. But when you're fifteen and your boyfriends nearly twenty-three, people don't approve. Does everyone really assume that all young people can't be trusted? Nikki had no interest in boys her own age, they seemed childish, and it made perfect sense to her to be with someone older. It wasn't about sex, she was too young for that. It was about friendship and feeling loved.

Steve and Nikki both knew that they loved each other. It wasn't a fling or a crush or anything like that, it was love. It had crept up on Nikki. She hadn't felt an overwhelming rush of excitement, like she had the first time she saw Pip at the hospital. She hadn't felt awkward or flustered. She felt happy, safe, cared for and desired - despite the ugly scarring on her legs- and, above all, she felt loved. She didn't want to ever be apart from him and whenever she was, she counted the hours until she would see him again. When he went home for the Easter break, she was devastated. Their relationship had become intimate and passionate but not to the extent of inappropriate for a girl of her age. It stopped just short of that, but only just. They both wanted to take things further and had talked about it and were both prepared to wait until Nikki was sixteen.

On Easter Sunday Mrs Edwards gave Nikki a chocolate egg Steve had left for her.

"It's from Steve," she said as she handed it to her daughter. "Isn't that nice of him?" Nikki wasn't that impressed. He had been gone for over a week and, apart from an obviously hurried postcard, she hadn't heard from him. To be honest she was feeling more than a little let down. That was until she opened the egg. Inside lay a silver cross and chain necklace and a note which read,

"My darling Nikki, I am so sorry I can't be with you at Easter, but remember I am thinking of you and can't wait to be back with you soon. I love you. Steve xx"

Nikki started to cry. Her parents looked at each other.

"Has he upset you?" asked her mother.

"No," said Nikki, "he loves me".

"Don't be ridiculous," said Marion, more than a little surprised. "He's twenty-three!"

"I shall be having words with that young man when he gets back," said her father. Nikki wished she hadn't let on to what the note said. She took herself off to her room. She wasn't going to let them spoil this.

Mr Edwards <u>did</u> have words with Steve on his return, much to Nikki's embarrassment, but it made no difference to their relationship. Steve openly admitted to her parents that he did indeed love their daughter and that he could fully understand their reservations due to the age difference. He seemed a lot older to Nikki as she sat on the stairs listening to the two men chatting in the kitchen. The conversation was open and frank. They discussed morals and what is deemed acceptable behaviour.

Nikki couldn't quite believe what she was hearing. She was glad not to have been in the room as she would have died of embarrassment. Having said tha,t she felt very proud of Steve. She admired his honesty and openness and she loved him all the more for it.

The two of them were inseparable, Steve became one of the family and when the time came for him to go home for the summer, Mr Edwards offered to drive him and his belongings back to his family home. After nearly nine months together, Nikki was going to met Steve's parents.

Big mistake.

They hit the roof. Angry that he had been dating anyone whilst he was supposed to be studying at an expensive college, it was bad enough he had been wasting his time on a youth club let alone anything else, but to be dating a child, a <u>disabled</u> child at that, what on earth was he thinking? She would be no good for him and would hinder his career. That, coupled with the fact that Nicola and her family were not of their class, was all just too much.

Derek Edwards immediately went on his daughter's defence. It was a side of him Nikki had never seen before and she felt much protected in what quickly became a very uncomfortable situation. He told his wife and daughter they were leaving and left the house. Steve joined them outside.

"I am so sorry, so embarrassed," said Steve. "I thought they may be a little annoyed, which was why I hadn't told them, but I didn't expect that reaction, I really am sorry. They try and control everything I do, they say it's for the best, but the last few months with you all have been wonderful, not having them looking over my shoulder the whole time." Nikki was hurt and upset, particularly by Steve's mother's obvious contempt for her. She didn't feel like a child and resented the things she had implied. Steve promised to speak to his parents over the summer but as Nikki and her parents pulled out of the drive, she felt sure it wasn't going to do much good.

For the next couple of weeks, Nikki thought a lot about Steve and the things his mother had said. She was hurt but could also see her point of view, to an extent at least. Despite missing him, the summer holidays passed surprisingly quickly. Steve had started out writing a couple of times a week but as the time passed the letters became less frequent and less affectionate. They focused more on the great time he was having on his brother's boat and less on her. His parents were making damn sure he would fully understand exactly the sort of life style he would be giving up if he were to choose Nikki over their wishes. By the time September came and Steve returned to university, it was Nikki who decided to make it easy for both of them and suggested they should spend time apart. He definitely changed during the summer, but so had she. She had got some serious studying to do in her final year of school if she was to be in with any chance of passing her 'O' levels the next June. By October, they decided not to see each other again.

Although the parting was a tearful one, they both knew it was for the best.

Two months later, on her sixteenth birthday, the youth club planned a surprise party for her. Nikki was back in her wheel chair after yet another knee operation, albeit minor and the party was the first time she had been out in three weeks. She went along determined to enjoy herself. Everyone had made a real effort to make it special for her. *Desdin* tried their best to play '*Happy Birthday Sweet Sixteen*' which was special in itself. They were much more Quo than Sedaka, but Nikki appreciated the thought. One of the leaders came over to let her know that Steve was unable to be there but wished her a very happy birthday. Nikki felt a pang in her heart. She missed him. She was sixteen now, if they got back together, maybe their relationship could move on. She decided there and then that first thing in the morning she would write to him and explain how she felt.

She heard nothing from him for three weeks, and then a note fell out of a late Christmas card he sent to the family. None of what it said sounded very much like her Steve, especially the bit that said, *'A second bite of the cherry is never as sweet as the first'*. What the hell was that supposed to mean? But it was obvious. He really had moved on. He had been spending a lot of time at the Braithwaits. Steve's family and the Braithwait family were life-long friends. The links between them went back nearly two centuries. Steve had been working closely with the Lord Braithwait, who had got Steve lined up to take on the day- to- day running of the family estate. Sarah Braithwait had been a childhood sweetheart and both families had always assumed that he two of them would marry. It seemed that Steve's mother had got her way. The letter went on the say that he and Sarah were to be married as soon as he had graduated. This was obviously more than a little rushed as he was to be a father in the spring! Nikki felt numb. He must have been seeing Sarah, whoever she was, over the summer but hadn't the guts to tell her.

Bastard!

She had trusted him so completely.

That <u>really</u> hurt.

Chapter Three

Nikki left school in the summer of 1979. Her whole class enjoyed a fantastic party at one of the trendier teacher's homes. He had joined the teaching staff only a couple of years earlier after the school had moved towards a new way of teaching by sharing resources with the local polytechnic.

It was a new initiative scheme that only a handful of school's throughout the country had embraced. Quite forward thinking, for the time. Many local authorities considered the fast changing education system to be heading for disaster. But the scheme worked well at Nikki's school, or at least it appeared to. She and her friends were happy and most had achieved good grades. Still, what did she know about the politics of it all? Pretty much the same as any other sixteen year old, she imagined. Admittedly, some took an interest but Nikki, like many others, didn't.

Nikki worked hard on both her school work and her fitness levels and by the time she left school, she had achieved eight 'O' levels and her legs were pretty much working as they should. She was as ready for the party as anyone else.

The party started at lunch time with a barbeque. Mr Bradley, Jim, as they were all now allowed to call him, had the most amazing mid-terrace Georgian house. Four floors packed with music collectables from the fifties and sixties as well as wall-to-wall books that lined the hallways and landings. The main focus in this quite enchanting Aladdin's cave, was an original five foot tall, American Wurlitzer juke box. It had once been housed in a diner in the States. Jim had first seen it during his travels after graduating from Cambridge University in the early sixties. He didn't obtain it at the time, (only the diner sign from above the front door was smuggled home then) he had recently tracked it down through an auction house and just had to have it. It stood stately in a largish room on the first floor, which housed little else.

"Room to express yourselves," Jim told his very impressed young friends. Jim had been a breath of fresh air in the school. He always wore a black suit, off white shirt and a thin tie. He never really looked smart. He was just one of those 'messy' people. Unkempt blonde wavy hair, hung just below his collar and Nikki's mum, like many other parents, thought him unsuitable to teach their children, especially something as precious as English. This apparently, was only based on looks. Jim Bradley was a very likeable bloke and an instant hit with the students. Consequently they worked hard and the evidence was there for all to see. Although his teaching methods may have appeared a little unorthodox to some, when it came to exam results, not one of his students failed that summer.

"I still think that teachers should look like teachers,"

said Mrs Edwards, "and speak the Queens English, not all *yeah* and *groovy*." This always made Nikki laugh.

"Why can't he be more like that nice Mr Blackmore?" her mother continued "He's what you'd expect a respectable English teacher to be."

Nikki always suspected that her mother had a bit of a crush on Mr Blackmore. He was in his early fifties, quite nice looking with a wry smile and his eyes twinkled when he spoke. But he had the most boring voice and was not very engaging. Mr Blackmore was indeed, exactly how you'd expect a teacher to be, including the worn brown corduroy trousers, checked blazer with leather elbow patches and a green wool tie. He also had the worst halitosis, which, as any teenager will tell you, puts you right off the lesson that such an afflicted person may teach.

It wasn't until after the party when Nikki informed her mother that Mr Blackmore had turned up with one of the student teachers that he had apparently left his wife for, that Mrs Edwards withdrew her admiration for him.

Almost all of Nikki's thirty- two peers were at Jim Bradley house that day. It was the most amazing party. Up until then, parties for Nikki had been rather tame, mainly just family events and all a little 'samey'. This was far from that. Jim had laid on numerous silly childish games that everyone threw their heart and soul into. It was at this party that Nikki discovered people took substances for fun. Or so they thought. Nikki was by no means a square in any way but after years of being drugged up with pain killers and medication that had given her all sorts of side effects, including hallucinations and the feeling of being totally 'spaced out', she really didn't understand how choosing to put yourself in that situation, was fun. It just wasn't and despite pressure, even from some of her closest friends, she wanted no part of it.

Nikki really loved music. She had spent hours listening to huge variety during the months she had been laid up. Sometimes this had been her only distraction and consequently it had formed an important part in her life. Jim had the most amazing record collection. The vinyl's stacked in boxes, uniformly categorized from the late forties to present day. The sixties were obviously Jim's favourite period and very few artists were omitted from that period. What he didn't know about the artists wasn't worth knowing. Nikki and a few others sprawled out over the scatter cushions discussing with Jim the merits of rock'n'roll, The Beatles influence, glam rock and the more recently emerging, ugly face of punk. Well, Nikki thought it ugly. Jim however, saw it as a positive development in young people's expression of the time and that had to be a good thing. After a couple of hours she felt almost convinced she should be enjoying this genre. She didn't, but Jim still put forward a good argument.

The conversation was interrupted by a loud announcement in the hallway that the cavalry had arrived. This was in the form of John Rowland and Tom Jones. Everyone had always found it highly amusing that the boy's sports department was run by this double act. It was especially funny that any teacher should be called *Tom Jones* as he also taught Music. As well as PE, John Rowland taught Woodwork. Nikki had been taught this subject to 'O' level standard. She had enjoyed these classes immensely and John had been a tremendous support, ensuring she was able to complete work she may have fallen behind with due to her treatment. In addition to the extra help he had, on occasions, even given her lifts home during her time in the wheel chair. This had resulted in him developing his friendship with her sister Suzanne. Others may have found it embarrassing their sister was dating a teacher, Nikki didn't. John was a good bloke. But the thing Nikki liked best about John was his friend from teacher training college, Mick Ford. He was handsome, sporty and <u>very</u> fit. Nikki had met him whilst he was staying with John a few weekends earlier. She, Suzanne, John and Mick had all met up for a picnic. John and Suzanne had brought a badminton set along with them and as they went to set it up, Nikki was left alone with Mick to chat and clear up the picnic things. There was an obvious attraction between them and before long the picnic blanket had become a welcome layer between them and the grass beside the river. Mick confessed to Nikki that it was John's idea about the weekend and the double date. Nikki didn't know whether to be more surprised that a teacher was fixing her up, or that John and Suzanne would think it – or <u>she</u> – would be that easy! As it turned out, she was rather pleased. Mick was a hunk, and he knew it, but so did Nikki and she really liked him.

By the time John and Suzanne returned to the river bank, Mick and Nikki were locked in each other's arms, oblivious to their surroundings.

John Rowland and Tom Jones bounded into the room where Jim, Nikki and the others were crashed on the floor. Both of them were dressed in 'Sergeant Pepper' outfits. They pulled Jim to his feet and whisked him away out of the room. It was obvious they were planning something.

After half an hour or so, the patio area at the foot of the long garden, burst into colour. Set up with a make shift stage, lighting and sound system that would have looked good in any club. There on centre stage were 'The Skool Levers' all dressed as the Beatles and performing extremely well rehearsed renditions of their hits. They were fantastic. The garden became a night club. But for Nikki, the best surprise there, on bass guitar was Mick. As soon as she saw him, her heart skipped a beat. It was a total surprise. He hadn't let on to her he was going to be part of this. Later he told her an even better surprise. Next term he would be joining the staff and also be house sharing with John.

"It'll be great," Mick continued, "we can be together properly now." He scooped her up in his arms and kissed her passionately. Nikki felt amazing. All the other girls screamed with excitement and cheered. Some of the boys muttered disapprovingly, probably out of jealousy but Nikki felt fantastic. She had never been short of attention from the boys in her year group or any boys come to that, but those her own age had never interested her. She liked them, well enough as friends but other than the mistletoe frenzy that appeared to be obligatory every December, she had never done anything more than hold hands on a walk around the town with any of them.

'The Skool Levers' played late into the evening and, by the time they started to pack up, many of the class had begun to drift away. I don't think any of them realized quite how final that day had made everything. The group that had got on so well together for the last five years, so much so, even the staff were sorry to see them go, were to be together no more. Some people would keep in touch, some friendships would remain for life, but as a group, all together, that was it. The last to leave the party was Tom Jones and he amused those left behind by singing *'Green Green Grass of Home'* as he made his way along the street. That left John, Suzanne, Mick, Nikki, Jim and his wife, Freya.

"Time for us to crash," said Jim as he and Freya started to make their way inside. "You guys can use the 'Diner'. Goodnight all."

Mick put his arm tightly round Nikki's waist. "Come on," he said, "let's get the best pitch."

They raced towards the house. Freya had made the 'Diner' look wonderful. The juke box lit the room as it played 'Rod Stewart's *'I Don't Want To Talk About It'* and the scatter cushions had been arranged into sleeping areas. Clusters of candles on silver platters flickered on the varnished wooden floor. Nikki thought it was beautiful. Now she found herself here with Mick, a gorgeous hunk of muscle who had surprised her earlier by moving to be near to her. It suddenly dawned on her that this could be the night. You know. <u>The</u> night! The one when you can't put off the inevitable any longer. The one when you run out of good reasons <u>not</u> too. The one when you stop fighting your feelings and go all the way. She hadn't imagined it would be like this, not in a teacher's house! That just wouldn't be right. But the setting was otherwise perfect. She was sixteen, she had left school, she felt safe and she loved Mick. Didn't she? The more she thought about it, the more she realized that actually, no she didn't. She liked him a lot, she fancied him and she liked being with him. He was a great kisser, he made her feel sexy and she felt special. He was an ideal boyfriend. Although at twenty-five, some of her friends thought him too old for her. But all in all, he was perfect. So <u>why</u> didn't she love him?

"I know what you're thinking, sweetheart," Mick said as he pulled her towards him "I'd love to too, but it's not the right time, not if we're dossing down next to your sister." As he said this, John and Suzanne came into the room just as the juke box played Rod Stewarts *'Tonight's the Night'*. Mick cuddled Nikki and they burst out laughing.

"What's so funny?" asked John.

"I'll tell you tomorrow," replied Mick. "Me and Nik have baggsied this corner."

Nikki and Suzanne left to find the bathroom.

"You're alright about this," Suzanne asked her sister as they made their way back to the room.

"Yeah. It's fun! Does mum know we're staying?" asked Nikki.

"She's fine about it, John promised to look after us, that was good enough for her." said Suzanne.

The two girls giggled as they went into the Diner to spend the night with the boys.

The next morning Suzanne and Nikki helped Freya prepare breakfast for Jim, Mick & John before he all helped to clear away the evidence of the previous day's party. There was an awful lot to do and it was midday before they even started on the garden.

Nikki didn't feel anything like a school girl anymore. She was with friends, not teachers, and having the best time. At three o'clock Jim announced it was 'time to go time', a regular phase he used to clear the class room at the end of a lesson. Today, however, it indicated the time to go to the local pub.

Suzanne & Nikki eventually arrived back home around ten that evening. To Nikki's amazement their mother just asked if they'd had a good time. Mrs Edwards had always been very protective of Nikki, understandably, but now she was beginning to let go a bit and Nikki felt free. Free from school, free from hospital, free from patronizing sympathy but above all free from the fear that she couldn't lead a <u>normal</u> life. She could. And she had started to do just that and was enjoying every minute of it.

Chapter Four

The summer of '79' spent with Mick was great fun. Together with John and Suzanne, they spent lazy days on the beach, visiting city museums and galleries, went to concerts and hardly spent a moment apart. Nikki was having the time of her life. John and Suzanne's relationship had moved on somewhat and they were quite serious about each other. Nikki and Mick were the best of friends and although Mick wanted to take it to the next level, Nikki didn't. She wasn't ready for that yet. She also felt that when the time came, she wanted it to be with someone she really loved, and although she really cared about Mick, he felt more like a big brother now. Mick was great; a little frustrated maybe, but understanding nevertheless. He just thought she needed a bit more time and was surprisingly patient. Nikki worried a little that if she didn't sleep with him he might leave to find someone else that would. Like Steve had. But that wasn't a good enough reason and if he chose to do that, he wasn't worth staying with anyway. The truth was she didn't love him, they were friends and that was that.

The fourth week of the summer holidays, John and Mick

were off to help at an adventure holiday for children from a variety of disadvantaged backgrounds. It was something they had got involved in during their time at University. The children came from all walks of life; some from less-well-off families, who would otherwise never had the opportunity to go on holiday, some suffering from low self esteem and confidence and others recovering from debilitating illnesses and conditions. It was challenging but rewarding and something the two men had done every summer for the last four years. This year they were returning to a water sports holiday centre in Derbyshire.

"Come with us." Mick asked Nikki as they sat in the pub garden only days before they were due to leave.

"It's a bit short notice,' replied Nikki "But it sounds great, I'd love to, if you think it will be ok?"

"I can teach you to canoe," said Mick excited at the prospect of her accompanying him on the trip.

"Why don't we *all* go?" asked Mick turning to Suzanne.

"No chance," said Suzanne "You won't get me in a canoe, and anyway, it's not a good time for me, not with the business just starting up."

Suzanne was not at all the sporty type. She was well manicured and very conscious of her image. She had experimented with a number of hair styles and both she and Nikki had suffered *disastrous* perms the previous year. Suzanne had just qualified as a hairdresser and had been working in a small salon, in a village eight miles out of town. John had encouraged her to 'go it alone' and at the end of June she had done just that. She was yet to find her own premises but in the meantime she was establishing a regular round of customers through home visits. This was proving to be a great success but extremely time consuming and Suzanne knew that the only way to reach her goals was to give the project her full commitment.

"Fair enough," said Mick. "You'll still come though, won't you Nik?"

"Yes, if you're sure it'll be okay with everyone else?"

"Great," said Mick "I'll give them a call in the morning"

Saturday morning came and Mick picked Nikki up from her home at eight. Everyone was making their own way there and the participating children would be arriving from all over the country at various times, for various lengths of stay.

As soon as she arrived, Nikki was greeted by Jo. She was the site manager and the co-ordinator of the trip. The site was used through term time for school trips; management team building exercises as well as various coaching and training camps. The whole place was vast, covering more than forty acres, of which the central point was a beautiful large lake that hosted a huge variety of birds despite being used for water sports. The main building had a large communal dining area, a log cabin style soft seating area which was lit up in the cold evenings by an enormous open fireplace. Most of the guests slept in small huts scattered around the edge of the first field which although basic, were a tad more comfortable than sleeping under canvas. There were also a couple of twelve- bed dormitories, as well as eight double luxury cabins for those guests who preferred not to rough it quite so much. These also had their own en suite facilities; everybody else had to use the shower and toilet block at the top of the field.

"The kids will start to arrive tomorrow," said Jo "Today we need to finalise the activity time table and delegate areas of responsibility."

Jo was very efficient, -some might have thought her bossy- but Nikki liked her. She was a single woman of about thirty; a slim, sporty type with wavy brown hair and very passionate about her work. Jo liked Nikki too and paired her up with herself to supervise the following afternoons raft building challenge.

Mick and John met up with old friends and everyone seemed to gel so well together. Nikki felt like she'd always been part of the team.

"Only one more for you to meet," said Jo towards the end of the team briefing. Just as she said this, the cabins large, creaky wooden door flew open.

"Sorry I'm a bit late, have I missed anything?"

"Only all the hard work." jested Jo as she stood up to greet her friend.

"For the new ones amongst us," she said "This is Philip, Pip to his friends."

Nikki couldn't believe her eyes. She couldn't believe her heart either as it thumped in her chest.

It was him, Pip, the guy she had met in the physiotherapy department four years earlier. Whatever it was, that had made her feel the way she did that day, it was happening again. This time she knew what it was. It was love, or maybe lust or probably both. All she knew for sure, was from that first meeting to this, she had never felt that way about anyone else. She really hoped that neither he, or Mick would notice.

Pip nodded round acknowledging everyone, he lingered slightly when he saw Nikki as if he recognised her, but he just smiled and said 'hello'. After briefly filling Pip in on the things he'd missed, the meeting concluded and everyone started to mingle less formally. Mick asked Nikki if she wanted to go to the local pub for some real ale with John and a couple of the others.

"You don't have to," butted in Jo "stay here with the girls if you like. We can all get to know each other a bit better."

"Sounds good to me," chipped in Pip as he jumped onto a large shapeless sofa "I'm more than happy to stay with the girls," Nikki could see that everyone liked Pip. He was funny, flirty and something endearing about him that few men posses. It was a sort of 'little boy' innocence. He must have noticed that women hung round him but didn't show any sign of conceitedness. The men liked him too, he was just one of those people that everyone wanted to be with. And Nikki was one.

"Hello again," said Pip, "Sorry if I stared at you earlier, have we met before?" Nikki could believe he recognized her; it had been four years since they had met and even then, the meeting was brief.

"Yes," she replied "I'm Nikki Edwards. I'm amazed you remember me. I was supposed to go one of your rehab camps but didn't make it in the end."

"Really? Where were we supposed to go?" asked Pip.

"Norfolk."

"Oh I remember," said Pip "You stood me up."

"No, you stood *me* up," smiled Nikki "I only met you that once. I didn't get the chance to tell you I was able to go, let alone the chance to then say I couldn't!"

"Just as well, it wouldn't have done for you to see a

grown man cry," joked Pip "Anyway you're here now, how did you get involved with this motley crew?"

Nikki felt awkward. She didn't want to tell him about Mick, not just yet anyway, but she didn't have to, Jo bounced down on the sofa beside Pip.

"So how do you two know each other" she asked?

"We don't. Not really," said Nikki "we only met once, a long time ago" Nikki didn't want to tell Jo where she had met Pip. She hated explaining to people the problems she had endured in the past; it was boring and distracted from what was relevant now – the present.

"Oh how *cruel*" cried Pip clutching his heart. "This young woman walked into my life one day and then just left me, never to be seen again until today."

"Oh yeah? When was that?" asked Jo.

"Four years ago," answered Nikki "I was all of twelve."

"You must have been an amazing twelve year old," smirked Jo "Pip meets hundreds of kids"

"And now she's an amazing sixteen year old" said Pip, he winked at Nikki and she felt herself blush.

"Can I get you both a top up?" asked Nikki indicating to their glasses.

"I'd rather have a coffee" said Pip.

"Is it ok to put the kettle on?" asked Nikki "I'll make it."

"Make yourself at home," said Jo.

Nikki went into the kitchen area.

"I can't believe you remember a girl of twelve you met once Pip, there must be more to it than that" quizzed Jo.

"Joanna! Whatever are you implying! I used to be a volunteer at the *Bright Future Charity* that helps disabled youngsters before I helped to start up *Challenge Everyone.*" replied Pip.

"Is Nikki disabled then? You'd never know." said Jo somewhat surprised.

"No" said Pip, "That's just the point. She was one of those kids who would have slipped through the net. Nikki went through years of surgery and physiotherapy and would have benefited from the sort of opportunities that other kids were offered. But because she wasn't registered as disabled, she wasn't given the same chances that could really aid recovery. So I bent the rules slightly and started to included kids, just like her, on the holidays and trips. The charity threatened to withdraw funding. It seemed so unfair, so I decided to start my own thing. Bit by bit, the rest of you got on board and the rest, they say, is history" Pip smiled.

"Coffee?" interrupted Nikki "Sugar anyone?" The three of them sat and chatted about the cabin and the campsite outside and Nikki felt right at home.

"You didn't tell me how you got involved with this lot." said Pip.

"She's here with Mick" leaped in Jo before Nikki had the chance to reply.

"Oh really?" questioned Pip "That randy 'ol bugger" Nikki looked a little shocked.

"I'm sure he has his moments," said Nikki "We're just friends."

Why did she say that? Was it true? Just because she hadn't actually slept with Mick, didn't mean they weren't a couple. Maybe she had just realized, she didn't *want* to be a couple.

Either way she wasn't sure if she should have said it and she felt very uncomfortable.

"Is that so?" said Pip "Make sure he realizes that, he's got a bit of a reputation"

"I will." said Nikki.

John and the others arrived back from the pub. Mick was last through the door..... with Rosie. She had arrived late and had met the boys in the pub. Mick looked at Nikki.

"This is Rosie," he slurred "She's from our college, didn't think she was coming this year so........." Mick stopped. Was he really going to say '*so I brought you instead?*'

"Hi Rosie," beamed Nikki not quite knowing what else she could do "I'm Nikki, a friend of John and Mick's from school."

"Nice to see you again, Rosie" interrupted Pip. "Hey Mick, fancy you bringing Nikki along this year. We go way back, don't we love?" he smiled at Nikki and made her heart melt. He had rescued her from total embarrassment. And the others come to that.

"Well, time for us all to retire, I believe," Pip continued, "early start tomorrow. Goodnight all. Come on Nikki, I'll walk you to your hut, its pitch black out here."

"Thanks," said Nikki relieved to get out of the cabin "Goodnight everyone."

"See, told you she'd be okay about things. It's fine" they heard Mick slur as they closed the door. John was furious with Mick and stormed off out the cabin, nearly bumping into Nikki and Pip as he fumbled for a torch.

"Sorry, Nikki, you didn't deserve that, Mick's an arse, are you okay?" he said.

"I'm fine, John, really. Mick and I are friends. I don't want any more than that, he knows that."

"Suzanne told me to look after you." said John.

"And you are John, but I really don't need you too, I can look after myself."

"And if all else fails, I'll look after you too." said Pip grinning broadly.

"Aarrh, watch him Nik, he's old enough to be your father." laughed John. He bid them both goodnight, before disappearing off into the darkness. Nikki and Pip started to make their way across the field.

"Are you?" asked Nikki.

"Am I what?" replied Pip.

"Are you old enough to be my father?"

"Dunno, how olds your father?"

"Forty- eight."

"Then no, I'm not" he laughed.

"You know what I mean, how old are you?"

"I'm thirty five. Bet that seems ancient to a sixteen year old?"

"Not really, it depends on the person. Some people are old by the time they're twenty, others can still be very childish at fifty."

"Wise words from one so young." smiled Pip

As they arrived at the hut that Nikki would be sharing with a couple of the other female leaders, Pip asked her if she really was okay.

"I'm fine, really, thank you. And thank you for walking me *home*." she grinned.

"My pleasure. Goodnight sweetheart." Pip said kindly.

"Goodnight Pip, see you in the morning." As she shut

the door, she couldn't wait to see him again and this time she only had to wait a matter of hours.

The camp started to come to life around seven the next morning. The smell of sizzling bacon wafted across the dew kissed field, as slowly one by one people began to emerge from the huts. Some raring to go and others, like Mick, a little worse for wear. Mick waited for Nikki as she left the shower block.

"I'm sorry, Nik, I didn't know Rosie was going to turn up." he said sheepishly.

"Would that have made a difference then?" asked Nikki.

"Ex- girlfriend. It all got a bit messy, but she wants me back, which is a *lot* more than I deserve. I know I've put you in an awful position and understand if you want to go home?"

"You've gotta be kidding Mick, I'm not going anywhere. Look, its fine, really, we both know we weren't going anywhere. Let's all try and get along and get on with the real reason we're here." said Nikki.

"You're amazing, Nik," said Mick and hugged her. "thank you, no hard feelings?"

"No Mick, I just wished you could have told me about her that's all."

"Sorry."

"Do you love her?"

"Yes, I think I do."

"Then go for it Mick, you only get one life. Be happy." Mick hugged her again.

"Thanks, Nik. Friends forever, promise?"

"Friends." said Nikki and she hugged him back just as Pip came round the corner of the shower block.

"Morning, Nikki. Is this ol' reprobate bothering you?"

"No, we just had to sort some stuff out, that's all. See you at breakfast."

Nikki sat with John and Jo at breakfast. Mick and Rosie came over to join them. John and Mick exchanged grunts and Nikki felt she needed to clear up the situation once and for all.

"It's Okay John. Let's move on. What's the plan for this morning?" asked Nikki.

"I'm taking you canoeing," said Mick "just as I promised. We won't get much chance once the kids start to arrive."

"Great," said Nikki and after breakfast, John, Rosie, Mick and Nikki made their way to the lake and Nikki's friend, taught her to canoe.

Chapter Five

"How do you know Pip?" asked Nikki as they paddled across the lake.

"Could ask you the same thing." replied Mick.

"You first."

"Through this scheme. He's a friend of John's, they met at college. John was doing his teacher training course and Pip was a tutor."

"Is Pip a teacher too?"

Mick laughed "No, he's a Chippy."

"A what?"

"Chippy; carpenter, self -employed, pretty good by all accounts. I thought you knew him?"

"I met him once, briefly, a long time ago, didn't really know him" Nikki realized she didn't know much about Pip at all, but what she did know she liked. She liked a lot.

Jo, Pip and some of the others came over to the edge of the lake.

"Lunch in half an hour" shouted Jo. Mick pulled the canoe out of the water and secured it to the jetty.

"How did you get on?" Pip asked Nikki as her foot sunk

into the mud up to her knee. Pip grabbed her life jacket to stop her falling backwards into the water. He pulled her towards him.

"Whoa, got you. That was close!" he laughed.

"Thanks," said Nikki "I think I did okay; it was fun. I might have to work on getting back on dry land though." She looked into his eyes and had to make conscious effort to break her gaze.

"She was great, a natural." called Mick "Baggsie Nik's in my team this afternoon."

"No, I want her in *mine*" replied Pip "we're raft building and John said she got her woodwork 'O' level, I could do with a skilled labourer," Nikki was enjoying the banter, she didn't mind what she did, she was having a great time.

"Aren't you the popular one......" said Jo in a tone that Nikki wasn't sure how to take. So she just smiled.

"I'll get out of these wet things and I'll come and give you a hand with lunch" she said and went off towards her hut.

"You'd better watch that one, Pip," Jo said as she walked with him back to the cabin

"What's that supposed to mean?" retorted Pip

"Just be careful that's all, she's very young. You must have noticed the way she looks at you?"

Pip laughed "I can't help it, I'm lovely," he said.

He really was innocent. Until Jo had suggested it, it hadn't crossed his mind that Nikki might fancy him. But now, he wondered if she did.

He found himself rather hoping she did.

The week flew by. Forty children of various ages and abilities took part in the programme and on the Friday evening, they concluded the activities by putting on a variety show to entertain each other. Pip was responsible for co-ordinating this. He was a natural. He played guitar, sang and was a gifted comic. He inspired everyone to give it a go. Pip was wonderful with the kids and everyone performed something, from poetry to dance acts, singing to magic. Mick, John and Pip always put a band together for the finale and this year was no exception.

"How's your singing Nik?" asked Pip.

"I love singing, but I've never sung in public before."

"We've been planning an attempt at '*Waterloo*'. Mick and John as Benny and Björn; I'll be Agnetha and you can be the other one. What's her name?"

"Frida,"

"Yeah her. You up for it?"

Nikki thought this would be really funny and jumped at the chance.

It was.

It brought the house down. The three men looked ridiculous in far too tight satin outfits. Nikki looked pretty good in hers, despite it being on the long side. The fact she had to spend most of the song trying not to trip over the bell-bottoms, only added to the comedic value. All four of them made the most of the wolf whistles. They performed like pros, keeping straight faces like it was the most natural thing in the world to be dressed as they were! They were really quite good.

After all the kids had gone to bed, the leaders all gathered together in the cabin for a well earned drink and a de brief of the week. There was also tomorrow's award ceremony to finalize. All the kids received a certificate of achievement, as well as funny awards that reflected the week's incidents. There was also the *people's choice* award that the kids voted for. This was for the leader who had inspired them most. This had gone to Pip for the last three years and was known amongst the leaders as the *Philip Scarrow* award.

"Okay everyone. Let's call it a night" said Jo "It's alright for you lot - you can all go home tomorrow, I've got seventy Scouts arriving Sunday morning."

"Oooh, so many men, so little time." joked Pip "Gotta admire your stamina, Jo."

Jo threw a cushion at him.

"Goodnight Philip, see you in the morning."

"Nik!" called Mick as they left the cabin "Me and Rosie are going to give Jo a hand to set up for Sunday. John said he'll give you a lift home. Are you OK with that?"

"Yeah, no problem, John told me at breakfast," said Nikki.

"Don't suppose he's got room for a little one?" asked Pip.

"Who?" said Nikki

"Me. I had to get the train here, had a problem with the van. That's why I was late."

"I don't see why not, I'll ask him," said Nikki really hoping he'd say yes.

He did.

Everyone was packed up to leave and the last thing to do was to present the awards. The parents stood proudly watching as each child received their certificate.

"And finally," announced John "The *people's choice* goes to .... well for the first time ever, this year, the award is shared between two leaders and goes to................ Philip Scarrow and Nikki Edwards!" All the kids clapped and cheered as Pip and Nikki collected their plastic trophy together. Pip grabbed Nikki's hand and held it high in the air. Nikki felt wonderful; this was the icing on the cake for her. The past week had been the best week of her life. As they took their places back in the circle, Pip squeezed her hand.

"You deserve that, sweetheart. The kids love you. You're a real asset to the team here. You will come again next year, won't you?"

"Try and stop me," Nikki smiled "I've had the best time." She looked round at her new friends. Jo had been watching the two of them and was feeling more than a little jealous. She leant towards Nikki,

"You do know he's married." she said with a sneer.

Nikki felt as though a dagger had pieced her heart. No, she hadn't known he was married. Neither, Pip or anyone else had mentioned it. She just assumed he wasn't.

"What, *who's* married?" asked Nikki is a way that tried to imply she had no idea what Jo was talking about.

"Philip. He's married with a daughter, so don't go getting any ideas. He flirts with everyone, you're no different. Just thought you ought to know. It's so obvious you fancy him"

Jo put on a big smile and went across to greet the parents.

"Bitch." thought Nikki. Why had she said that? Nikki felt deflated. But why? This was silly. She had had a great time, Pip was still a lovely bloke and the fact he was married didn't change that. It didn't alter the fact she fancied him either. It just meant that now, it could never be anything more than that.

The journey home was pretty uneventful. Nikki fell asleep after only a few miles. Pip sat in the front passenger seat of John's Mini Clubman. It wasn't the most comfortable of cars for any of them but Pip was grateful for the lift back. Nikki was curled up on the back seat with luggage packed around her. She felt safe, content and exhausted. John and Pip chatted about their college days and their work. After three and a half hours John pulled up outside Nikki's home, he pipped the car horn and Suzanne came running out.

"Missed you" John said as Suzanne jumped into his strong arms and they hugged each other tight. Nikki's parents came outside too, just as Nikki and Pip got out the car.

"You've got a good colour, have you had a good time love?" Marion asked her daughter.

"Fantastic" beamed Nikki, "Mum this is ...."

"Hello, Derek," said Pip as he walked towards Nikki's father, "how are you?" he added firmly shaking his hand.

"Good to see you, Pip. Where have you been with my daughter?" Derek laughed. Nikki looked stunned.

"You *know* my Dad?"

"He knows everyone Nik. Haven't you realized that, yet?" chipped in John.

"I do some work for him from time to time." Pip replied "Known him for years. And I believe we have met once, before Mrs Edwards, but at the time I didn't realize you were Derek's wife"

"Have we?" she questioned.

"He was the guy who organised the activity trips when I was in physiotherapy mum, you remember?" said Nikki.

"Oh that was years ago. I'm sorry, I didn't recognize you."

"That's okay. Nice to meet you again" smiled Pip

"Got time for a cuppa?" asked Derek

"I'd love one, if that's okay? We didn't stop on the way back, the roads were clear so we decided to keep going. Could do with a drink now though" said Pip.

"Did our Nik chat non- stop all the way back? I'm surprised you too boys are still sane!" joked Derek.

"No, she fell asleep, thank goodness," laughed Pip as the party went into the house. Suzanne hugged her sister.

"Are you alright, Nik? John told me about Mick, what a *rat*" said Suzanne.

"It's fine Suze. Really. That was last weekend, an awful lots happened since then. Mick and I are friend's, you know I didn't want any more than that. Well, not with *him* anyway!" Nikki grinned and followed the others into the kitchen.

After an hour or so of drinking tea and chatting about the past week, Pip got up to leave.

"I really must be going." he said. John stood up to offer his friend a lift.

"You've only just got home, son" said Derek, kindly "I can run Pip home."

"Please don't worry, I can walk from here" said Pip.

"It's no problem. Won't be long, love." Derek said to his wife as he and Pip went to leave the room.

"Thank you for your hospitality, Mrs Edwards." said Pip sounding a lot younger than he was.

"My pleasure, and please, call me Marion" she replied.

"Thank you Marion," smiled Pip "By the way, you should be very proud of your daughter. She was brilliant this week. I'm hoping she will consider helping out with future projects"

Marion looked at Nikki.

"I *am* proud of her Philip. She's an inspiration."

"She is that," said Pip. Nikki felt herself beginning to blush. "We're putting on a show this Christmas. You interested Nik?" Pip's enthusiasm was infectious.

"Count me in," beamed Nikki "As long as you promise not to wear that pink satin suit again."

"Oooooh, can't make promises like that, I'm afraid" he laughed. "I've give you a call nearer the time. Better go, don't want to keep your dad waiting. See you soon, Nikki. Bye, Mrs Edwards, -Marion-, lovely to see you again"

"Bye, Philip." said Marion

"See you soon." hoped Nikki.

"What a nice young man." said Marion as she collected the tea cups "You sound like you've had a wonderful time. I'm sorry Michael let you down. I hope you weren't too upset? I said to your father, you can do a lot better than him."

"Mick and I are just friends mum, that's all. Everyone seems to think he was the love of my life or something. He really wasn't." she kissed her mother on the cheek. "Is the water hot enough for a bath? She asked.

"Yes, I knew you'd want one. And I've made a shepherd's pie with cheesy topping for dinner. Your favourite."

"Thanks Mum. Missed you" said Nikki as she went up to the bathroom.

It was good to be home. As she lay in the bath Nikki reflected on the past week and the rest of the school holiday. It suddenly dawned on her that it wasn't holiday anymore, she had left school. She would seriously have to think about getting a job. Most of her friends had either already found employment. Some were going on to do 'A' levels and Nikki felt a little left behind. She had been used to that. It had been the story of her life up until this summer but not anymore. She really felt she had turned a corner and it was time to catch up, once and for all.

Monday she would look for a job.

Chapter Six

It was the smell of Sunday lunch that eventually woke Nikki. She turned to look at the bedside clock, 12.15pm. Her eyes widened, she'd been asleep for fourteen hours!

"Well, good afternoon sleepy head" said Marion as her daughter entered the kitchen.

"Why didn't you wake me?"

"You were worn out Nikki, but I think all that fresh air and the sleep has done you the world of good" said her mother.

"Lunch smells great, I'm starving" said Nikki.

"It's certainly given you an appetite too," smiled her mother. "Go and tell your father lunch is in half an hour. You know where he is."

Derek was where he always was on a Sunday morning, in his workshop halfway down the unkempt garden. A well trodden path ran parallel with the washing line and the girls would occasionally cut the grass if it got too long and they wanted to sunbathe, but apart from that, the outside of the property was left to its own destiny. It was over grown but still a family garden. Marion had planted various rose bushes over the years which now formed a dense barrier between their property and the neighbours. On warm summer evenings the scents from this beautiful floral display filled the air with the smell of a true English garden.

"Hi Dad," said Nikki as she entered the workshop.

"You're up then" said Derek "What time do you call this?"

Derek and Nikki had a great relationship; they obviously adored each other but chose to show it by constantly teasing and making fun of each other. Marion didn't really understand this and would often become annoyed with both of them, telling Derek not to be cruel and Nikki not to be rude.

"Lunch is in half an hour. What are you making?" asked Nikki.

"Just finishing off the jewellery box for our Suze birthday, I wanted to get it done by lunch"

"Ooh, let's have a look Dad?"

"No, you'll break it." he joked.

"It's beautiful. Not bad for an old man!" said Nikki. Her father was a real craftsman. He was also a perfectionist. The box was indeed beautiful with intricate carving on the lid which comprised the letter 'S' with an intertwining vine.

"If you're very careful you can cut out the velvet lining." said Derek as he indicated to the red cloth laid out on the workbench. "It's measured exactly so get it right."

Nikki looked at the cloth. She looked back at her dad and looked at the precise measurements on the paper beside it.

"Better not," she said, "I'd hate to mess it up."

"No, maybe not," he laughed, remembering the last

time he let his daughter help him. It really wasn't her fault. She was left- handed and as any left hander will tell you, however hard you try to cut in a straight and accurate line, the scissors will choose their own route. Derek just thought she didn't take enough care.

"I told you it's the stupid scissors- not me" she said trying to defend herself. To which he replied *'A bad workman always blames his tools'* Years later Nikki purchased left-handed scissors and could prove her point, but Derek wouldn't have any of it.

"Tell mum I won't be long." said Derek as Nikki left the workshop.

The roast was cooked to perfection, as was the norm for Marion. John arrived right on dishing up time and the five of them all enjoyed the meal. The conversation revolved around Suzanne's business and her father made a number of suggestions that proved to be very useful to her. Derek had been running his own D.I.Y shop for the last fifteen years. He had previously worked for a much larger store in his late teens and early twenties after finishing his national service. He had learnt a number of skills, from plumbing to electrics, painting and decorating, but his real talent lay in carving and joinery. Derek had been encouraged to develop his skill, by a much older man who worked in the store. A true 'old- fashioned craftsman and dying breed', Derek called him. When the old man died, Derek felt the heart had gone out of the shop and a lot of changes were made. It was almost a tribute to him that Derek started his own business. Although sometimes finding it difficult to compete with the immerging superstores, he prided himself on something they couldn't offer. Time,patience, and the personal touch.

"It's quality, not quantity that people value. There's a place for all of us in this market" He was right, to an extent. His business was steady but he was never going to make a fortune. But, then again, that wasn't what was important to him.

As the plates were being cleared away, Derek turned to Nikki.

"So, my girl, how are you planning to make your mark on the world?"

"Not sure yet, but I intend to get a job of some sort this week, while I decide. I need to get some money from somewhere." replied Nikki casually.

"Yes you do, don't expect us to carry on paying for everything, your mum could do with a bit of rent off you now you've left school."

Nikki hadn't thought of that, she meant she needed money to go out, get some new jeans and there was a number of LP's she wanted. But she forced a smile at her father and her reply came out as "*yeah I do realize that*".

"We've got to treat you both the same, Suzanne got her first two weeks free and so will you after that you give your mother a half of what you earn for your board and keep." continued Derek. This seemed a bit steep but at the time it was hypothetical as she wasn't earning anything at all.

"So sweetheart, where are you going to look for this job," asked Marion "I don't think it will be as easy as you think, people don't just tend to walk into jobs these days."

"Oh I dunno, I thought I'd go into town tomorrow, I quite fancy working in a record shop or something." replied Nikki. "Lyn's Saturday job has just been offered to her full time in *Meanz Jeanz*. I'm meeting her for lunch tomorrow so maybe she'll know of somewhere."

Marion smiled at her daughter carefree optimism. She was proud and relieved that Nikki had such confidence in herself. After all her treatments, it could have been so different.

"Oh that's nice." said Marion "How is Lyn? You two haven't met up for some time, have you?"

"She's fine, I think. She's been seeing some boy called Tam. He's an idiot but she can't see it. You can't tell people, can you? You just have to be there when you're needed to pick up the pieces where it all goes wrong. Honestly mum, he's sixteen going on twelve, and soooo childish. Lord knows what she sees in him"

Marion smiled "Sometimes Nikki, I think you're wise beyond your years," she said fondly.

Chapter Seven

"Cup of tea." Derek said gently as he put the cup on her bedside table.

"What time is it?" asked Nikki.

"Seven o'clock. Early bird catches the worm, up and at 'em girl, I thought you were job hunting?"

"Thanks dad, I am," she said as she turned over and pulled the cover over her head.

"Don't leave it too long," said Derek as he left for his shop.

By nine fifteen, Nikki was on the bus making her way to town, determined that by the time she returned home that day she would have a job. She got off the number nine outside the railway station and started to make her way to the centre of town. She amused herself by picturing herself in various jobs. Train driver? Ha! no. Traffic warden? Never. She liked being popular. Taxi driver? No, she couldn't drive! And then, there in front of her was the *Railway View* hotel. This could be it. Receptionist? Chambermaid? Something. Anything, for the time being. This was worth a shot. She went up the stone steps that lead to the large entrance.

Entering the main lobby she rang the reception bell and a very camp middle-aged man popped up from behind the counter.

"Who's that pinging my bell?" he said in a voice that made Nikki want to laugh.

"Me," she beamed "I'm Nikki Edwards and I was wondering if you'd know of any jobs going at the moment. Here I mean, not worldwide" she laughed.

"Well, Nikki Edwards, this just might be your lucky day. It is already of course - you've just met me, but things could get even better. I know, is that possible? Anyway, one of the girls walked out last night, bit of an altercation with a long term guest. It got very messy, quite literally, she threw his dinner in his lap! The upshot is, she left us right up swan creek."

Nikki instantly liked this funny little man. Danny was in his early forties. He stood about five foot six tall, was very slim and his features were quite drawn. Nikki thought he looked like he could do with her mothers' cooking for a couple of weeks. His neat black hair was peppered with grey and his dark eyes sparkled. His deep smile lines were the evidence from years of being polite to people. They gave him the sort of looks that made you want to smile right back at him.

"Oooh, how rude am I? *Very* if you play your card right! Ha!" Danny winked in an exaggerated way and threw his hands into the air as if to punctuate his laugh. "I haven't introduced myself. I'm Danny the concierge........" He looked up to the ceiling and started counting on his fingers, "Head receptionist, bar-man, trolley-dolly, fashion advisor, peace- maker, general dog's body and all round good egg. Have a seat, luscious lass; let's see what *we* can do for *you*."

Danny practically skipped off through the large oak doors that led to the main dining area. After a few minutes he reappeared with a kindly looking, rather round lady in her late fifties.

"Mrs Pyke, this is Nikki Edwards," said Danny as though he was presenting her to the Queen. "She was wondering, if might be able to offer her any employment?"

Mrs Pyke smiled at Nikki. "Nice to meet you. Have you got any experience in the hotel trade?" She suspected the answer to be *no* as Nikki was so young.

"No, none at all, I'm afraid." said Nikki, and quickly added, "But I'm keen to learn."

"That's just what I like to hear, on both counts my dear," said Mrs Pyke kindly "A blank canvas for us to train the *Railway View* way."

Danny rolled his eyes in Nikki's direction and smiled back at Mrs Pyke before she noticed.

"I'll leave you lovely ladies to it then," he said "So much to do. Ping me before you leave, hen." "He's a lovely chap, wouldn't hurt a fly. Bent as a nine bob note mind, but lovely all the same." said Mrs Pyke. "Now let me give you a bit of a tour. We can chat at the same time and see if we can't sort you out with something."

Nikki was taken through the oak doors into the dining room, shown the bar and lounge area and then through to the kitchen, laundry and storage rooms. At the back of the kitchen was a small room - more like a cupboard than room- which Mrs Pyke referred to as her office.

"Cram in," she laughed "take a seat. Well my dear, do you think you'd like to join our little team?"

Without giving it hardly any thought, Nikki replied instantly, "Yes, Mrs Pyke, I think I would."

"We've got three part-time positions at the moment, - well four actually but one's behind the bar and you're too young for that - otherwise there's chambermaid, waitressing or catering assistant. What do you fancy?"

Nikki couldn't believe her luck. Not only had she found work in the very first place she looked, but had been offered a choice of jobs. The people seemed really nice. This was great.

"Actually, I was really looking for a full time position." said Nikki.

"Oh I didn't realize that, lovie." Mrs Pyke looked thoughtful and Nikki thought she'd blown it.

"Well, we can put the chambermaid and waitressing jobs together. Forty hours a week. There's a starting rate of twenty two pounds, plus any tips, uniform and one meal per shift. Hours to suit the business, which obviously means evenings and weekends. You will need to be flexible about that. How does that sound? Any questions?"

"No, I don't think so" Nikki was excited, if not a little naive.

"We just need you to complete a form then" continued Mrs Pyke. She leant over and lifted a thick folder out of the desk drawer. Nikki filled out the details as requested, but hesitated when it came to the medical questions.

1. *Have you had any illness or condition that has deemed you unfit for work for more than four weeks at any one time?*

54

2. *Have you any on-going medical condition?*
3. *Have you ever had an operation?*
4. *Are you diabetic?*
5. *Do you have a heart condition?*
6. *Do you smoke?*
7. *Do you drink alcohol regularly?*
8. *Do you have any hearing difficulties?*
9. *Do you wear glasses?*
10. *Does anyone in your family suffer from any mental health problems?*

If you have answered 'yes' to any of the above please give full and detailed information of the attached paper provided.

"Don't worry too much about that, lovie." said Mrs Pyke, "Most of it won't apply to a school leaver, unless you're smoking sixty a day!" she laughed.

Nikki gave a nervous smile before answering *no* to every question. If she had gone into great detail about her leg problems they would never offer her a job. Mrs Pyke had already explained that the job entailed an awful lot of standing and she could walk miles each shift. Nikki had assured her that it wouldn't be a problem. If she told the truth it would complicate things. And anyway, she was fine now. She knew she shouldn't have lied and she felt very guilty but she couldn't go back now.

"That's that, then" smiled Mrs Pyke "Just need to agree your start date. When can you start?"

"As soon as you want me" replied Nikki.

"Come in Friday for your induction and I can sort your uniform out then. You won't be paid for that mind. We can start you proper on Monday, eight o'clock. How does that sound?"

Thank you very much Mrs Pyke, I'm looking forward to it, I won't let you down."

"Welcome aboard, lovie. See you Friday" said Mrs Pyke as she rose to see Nikki out.

There was no-one about as Nikki walked back through the dining room and into the foyer. *Ping ping ping* went the desk bell and it made Nikki jump.

"I hope you weren't going to leave without 'pinging' me" said Danny "How did you get on?"

"I start Monday." grinned Nikki.

"Oh thank God for that, I need a bit of sunshine in my life. Looks like I've just been sent some" Danny took Nikki's hand and kissed the back of it before backing away with a theatrical swooping bow and bidding her *adieu*.

It was getting on for eleven and Nikki wasn't meeting up with Lyn for another hour or so, so she headed to the market. One of her school friend's brothers ran a record stall. He always gave her a discount and Nikki enjoyed talking about the latest releases with him. She found Andy enthusing with a couple of young lads about the new Elvis Costello Album. Nikki wasn't that familiar with his music except '*I can't stand up for falling down*' which she was teased with at school.

"Oi, Nik," Andy shouted "Put the cans on" Nikki put the enormous headphones on that Andy threw at her and was blasted with '*Accidents will happen*'

"Brill, ain't it." shouted Andy "I can let you have it for £1.99"

Armed forces was a really good LP and Nikki bought it.

"You busy later?" asked Andy

."Yes, quite. I'm meeting Lyn for lunch," said Nikki

."I meant tonight, I thought we could listen to some vinyls."

"I'm sorry, Andy, not tonight, maybe some other time. See you later. Thanks for the album." she said as she headed off to meet her friend. Andy was a nice lad but not at all Nikki's type.

"You look pleased with yourself" said Lyn as she emerged from the jean shop. "Have you had a good morning?"

"Got myself a job" grinned Nikki.

"Really? Well done you. Where?

"The *Railway View* hotel. You are looking at their newest chambermaid and waitress"

"How much." asked Lyn

"Twenty two pounds a week plus tips"

"Are you happy with that?"

"Yeah. Why?" Nikki began to wonder if she was being exploited.

"It's twenty four pounds a week here plus five percent discount on purchases"

"I think I might be better off then." said Nikki

"Guess you might be, if you don't mind all those one night only dirty 'ol business men drooling over you. You could flirt outrageously and be on to a nice little earner!"

"Well, if you've got it...." laughed Nikki. The two girls sat in the window of the *Wimpy* burger bar, chatting and laughing without a care in the world.

Nikki arrived home later that afternoon full of excitement with the prospect of her new job. She was a sensible young woman who wanted to make her own way in the world. Until she decided which career path to choose, she would support herself and gain some life experience. It might help her to decide what she really wanted to do. Her father didn't see it like that.

"You're so much better than that, Nikki" he said. "What on earth possessed you to take a job like that?"

"I'm not planning on staying there forever, Dad. It's ideal for me at the moment though"

"How much are they paying you?"

"Twenty- two pounds a week."

"Bloody slave labour if you ask me."

"Plus tips, I thought that was quite good." said Nikki trying to defend her decision.

"Well we all know how *tips* are picked up in that sort of establishment, don't we?"

"Derek" snapped Marion "That's enough, give her *some* credit, she a sensible girl. Let's just see how it goes, shall we?"

"Thanks mum" said Nikki as she went upstairs. What had she done that was so wrong? She thought they'd be pleased. She'd got a job, just like she said she would. She was proud of herself even if they weren't. And anyway, it was only a stop gap.

Her parents knew they had upset her by the sheer volume of *'Oliver's Army'* blasting from her bedroom.

Chapter Eight

"Well that's us done for the week." said Danny as he flopped back into the large leather armchair in the now deserted bar of the hotel. "How's your legs hen?" he asked Nikki, who had plonked herself down next to him. How did he know about her legs?

"What do you mean" she asked

"They must be killing you, if your feet haven't already beaten them to it."

"Oh, they're okay. My feet ache, but otherwise I'm fine" said Nikki.

"I couldn't help noticing your calf muscles. Wow -wee, you've got some strong 'ol pins there lovie. Bet you've got one hell of a grip!" he said giving her a knowing look and pulling a funny face.

"That's for me to know Danny and you ain't going to find out" she laughed.

"Come here you. Give your Uncle Danny a hug. I hope you've enjoyed your first week in *Fawlty Towers*. You and me, are going to be the very best of friends, I can feel it in my waters. Now, how are you getting home? It's your first late one tonight, isn't it."

"Dad's picking me up. I'd better see if he's outside. Thanks Danny, I've had a great week. See you Monday."

Derek Edwards pulled up outside the hotel, just as Nikki plodded down the stone steps.

"Hi Dad. Thanks for picking me up, I'm shattered."

"Well I'm not keen on you getting the bus this time of night. But don't think I'm going to make a habit of this either, I'm not a free taxi service, you may have to rethink this job." said Derek somewhat annoyed.

"Or learn to drive myself" chirped Nikki "Suze wants to sell me her car and get a little van for the business."

"Good grief, clear the roads, Nikki's got plans!" joked Derek "Don't think I'm going to teach you"

"I don't want you too, John's already offered."

"Sounds like you've got it all worked out. It'll take you a while to save up though, on twenty quid a week"

"Twenty- two. Plus tips."

"*Eleven*, once you've paid your mum. Did you get any tips this week? asked Derek.

"Yes."

"How much?"

"Nineteen pounds fifty!" beamed Nikki. Derek nearly swerved off the road.

"What did you do to get *that* sort of money?"

"I was polite, mainly. One old lady gave me five pounds just for getting her spoilt little dog a bowl of water."

"Was that it?"

"Pretty much, it soon adds up. Danny says a bad week for him is less than fifty quid, but he's the maitre de. He gets all sorts of other stuff too, theatre tickets, bottles of wine, that sort of thing. He's a right laugh too."

Derek could see that his daughter had enjoyed her first week at work. He was proud of her, he had only been concerned because he loved her so much and he didn't want to see his little girl being taken advantage of. However grown up Nikki thought she was, Derek knew she was still naive he wasn't sure she was ready for the big wide world. She was going to have to grow up pretty quick.

The first few of weeks at the *Railway View* Hotel flew by. Nikki soon proved to be a much welcome addition to the busy team and was enjoying her new job. She relished every new challenge. In addition to her normal duties of chambermaid and waitress, she had also helped out in the kitchen and on reception. Although not intellectually difficult, she found she thrived on the pressure that the job could bring, particularly at busy times. Everyone liked her, especially Danny and the two of them would often giggle their way through stressful moments. They grew very fond of each other.

"We were lacking something here until you arrived." Danny said to her over coffee one morning "Many think I still am!" he laughed.

"And my life was incomplete until I met you, I'm not sure what was missing but whatever it was, you've replaced my innocence with it!" Nikki replied with a grin.

"Are you implying I've lead you astray?" asked Danny trying to look hurt.

"I wouldn't *dare* suggest such a thing, but I have learnt a lot in the past few weeks, things I never knew went on, some thing's I wish I didn't know, went on."

"Darling, you ain't seen nuffin' yet!" Danny squealed as he jumped up to rinse the coffee mugs. "Has everyone been nice to you hen? Had any problems at all?

"No, everyone's been great. Except...." Nikki replied trailing off.

"Except what?"

"Except Pat. I don't quite know how to take her" answered Nikki. Pat worked in the kitchen, part time. She prepared vegetables and washed up. She was in her mid thirties, fairly plain looking, a bit frumpy and very loud.

"Oh God," said Danny rolling his eyes "Not many people *do* know how to take her. Think half her problem is that no one has *taken* her for some time! Has she been horrid to you, hen?"

"No" replied Nikki "She just, well just, oh I'm going to sound like such a snob."

"Spit it out, Nik"

"Well, she's so crude. She thinks it's funny to burp loudly and even funnier to pass wind! She acts like the boys from school. I just feel embarrassed being with her."

"I know what you mean. She'd show you up in public. You know, she's *begged* me time and again to be her toy boy, can you imagine, I think she was teasing but I'm never quite sure with her, she's far too touchy feely for my liking. I've had to beat her off with a stick!" said Danny.

"Really" Nikki was amazed.

"Don't sound so surprised. Beneath this calm and sensitive exterior, I can be quite ruthless, you know."

"No, I meant did she really ask you to be her toy boy? Not did you beat her off with a stick"

"Ooooh Nicola Edwards, you can be so cruel. Don't

question I could beat someone, oh no, but doubt that I could be the object of a women's desire! Well, thank *you*." Danny pretended to sulk.

"Sorry Danny. So why did you turn her down?"

"Vital bits missing, lovie" he laughed "That and the fact she's awful, not my type at all. Her husband, however, well he's another story. Bugger only knows how those two ever got together. What a waste!" Just at that moment Pat came into the rest room and flicked the kettle on. "Burr...p, s'cuse the pig. Who's been helping themselves to my coffee?" she asked.

"No one, we've got our own," said Danny. "Get a wiggle on Nikki, time we got up and at 'em."

Nikki and Danny went back into reception.

"Is there a special someone in your life, Nik? Danny asked as the two of them started to sort the recently returned laundry.

"Apart from you Danny? No. Not at the moment. You?"

"Well there's my Bernie, but he's like an old pair of slippers. We're just comfy, not sparkie, if you know what I mean. Sad 'ol things aren't we?"

"I don't feel sad, I've just finished with someone this summer." said Nikki.

"Oh I'm sorry, hen, you okay about it?"

"Yeah, we're friends. He was a bit immature to tell you the truth, we had fun but that was it, wasn't love or the real thing or anything like that."

"Listen to her, woman of the world! Seventeen going on forty- five" laughed Danny.

"Actually I'm not seventeen until next month."

"What date? he asked.

"Second of December, it's a Sunday."

"Let's have a look; if it's our weekend off we can have a bit of a party."

"Well I know *I'm* off" said Nikki, "I promised some friends I'd help with a Christmas show, kid's charity thing. Mrs Pyke wouldn't let me swap my evenings, so I'm taking my holiday then. Mind you, she made me promise to do extra cover over New Year to make up for it."

"Sounds great and I'll want to know all about it. Now, here we go." said Danny turning the pages of the reception diary, "You're in luck hen. Leave it all to me, party Saturday the first. You've got yourself a personal party planner!"

"Great stuff," Nikki smiled. "Well I'd better go and make the beds up. Thanks Danny, see you later."

Danny loved a good party. Any excuse to get dressed up. It didn't matter if it was Nikki's birthday or someone had left, or a friend of a friends long lost cousin was going to emigrate, Danny saw any and every occasion, as a good reason to party. He had been known to throw a party to celebrate the fact the packet of digestives he'd once had, were coated in chocolate, both sides! He thrived on planning surprises and knew so many people and contacts that the party wasn't going to cost him or Nikki, anything. The *Locomotive* pub, about four hundred yards along the road, had a function room above the main bar. Bernard, the spritely sixty eight year old barman, was a good friend of Danny's. They had kept each other company on many occasions and usually spent their Christmas's together. Danny always insisted they were 'just good friends' nothing more, but everyone knew there was more to it than that.

A finger buffet was prepared by the hotel kitchen

staff, without Mrs Pyke's knowledge, which was a bit of a challenge, but nothing they hadn't done in the past. Danny and Bernard decorated the function room with balloons and streamers and a large *Happy Birthday* banner.

Nikki had no idea how many people were going to be at the party. She arrived around seven o'clock, as per Danny's instruction, and was quite overwhelmed by his efforts.

"Oh Danny, this is wonderful. You are so kind, thank you" said Nikki and she hugged him.

"My pleasure hen" he said "but you need to thank our Berni" He turned to his friend to introduce him.

"So you're the famous Bernard?" said Nikki.

Berni raised his eyebrows. "Oooh am I? What's he been saying? You know you can't believe a word that comes out of that boy's mouth."

Nikki smiled "Thank you Berni, I really don't know what to say, you've both been so generous"

"You are most welcome, glad to hear you've been keeping my Danny in order."

"Ha ha, it'll take a lot more than me to achieve *that*." laughed Nikki.

The first guests started to arrive. Suzanne, John, Mick, Rosie, Lyn, Tam and staff from the hotel. Nikki's parents said they would pop in for an hour or so later, but they didn't like discos.

Nikki was having a great time, greeting everyone and having a laugh, when Pat came in. She made a bee line for Nikki. She just about wished her a happy birthday, before telling Danny she had let slip to Mrs Pyke about the food. Danny was never sure if she did this sort of thing in a vindictive way or she was just too thick to keep quiet.

Whichever it was it annoyed him. He went off to get some drinks.

Then, there stood Pip.

Nikki's heart leapt. She hadn't seen him for three months and although she was due to help with the concert next week, hadn't been able to be part of the preparation due to work. This meant she was now only going to be helping out front of house, showing people to seats and programme selling, rather than being *in* the show, which is what she would really have liked to do.

Nikki had hoped he might be at the party but only half expected him.

"Believe you know my 'ol man," said Pat as she swung round to Pip, "Small world isn't it?"

Nikki was stunned.

She couldn't believe it. How on earth would someone like Pip, funny, charming, popular and sexy be with someone so, well, so completely different?

"Happy Birthday Nik, fancy you working with Pat." said Pip. Nikki didn't know what to say.

"Yeah, fancy" she said. She could feel her face go taught as she stared at Pip in disbelief.

"Drinks people?" asked Danny as he re-appeared in a black waitress dress and white pinny. Thank God for Danny. He could break any embarrassing silence. Nikki and Pip roared with laughter.

"Now you," said Danny, handing Pat a glass of wine, "keep your hands to yourself tonight" He turned to Pip, "And you? Well, you on the other hand, can do what you like!"

Pip laughed even more.

"You're safe there" said Pat snidely "He's forgotten what he's got one for." This triggered another embarrassing silence.

The DJ muffled an announcement into the microphone. No one could really make out what he said, except for the end bit. *"especially for Suzanne & Nikki, the Foundations....."*

"Excuse me" said Nikki, "I love this song. Gotta find Suze, we always dance to this."

"Count me in" squealed Danny and they danced across the floor to meet up with Suzanne and the others, as the speakers boomed out, *'Build me up buttercup'*.

By ten o'clock the small room was heaving with people, many of which Nikki had never met before. Mostly they were friends of Danny's or friends of friends of Danny. Whoever they were, they were great fun and the party was a huge success. Nikki saw her parents over by the door. They had spent the last hour in the corridor trying to 'hear themselves think' as Marion put it. She was talking to John and Suzanne as Nikki made her way over to them.

"You off now?" asked Nikki.

"I don't know how you stand this." shouted Marion.

"We won't wait up," added Derek, "John said he'd see you home."

"Night, Dad." said Nikki and kissed him on the cheek.

"Be good. There are some right odd fellows in there. Just behave yourself." said Derek.

"I'll keep an eye on her." came a voice from behind her.

"Thanks, Pip. See you soon, goodnight."

Derek shook Pips hand and he and Marion left.

"Sorry about earlier. I didn't mean to embarrass you." said Pip.

"You didn't, Pat did. She often does. I had no idea she was your wife."

"Why would you have? I don't go bragging about it."

"Where is she now?"

"She's gone home. We only had a sitter until ten."

"How old's your daughter?"

"Carrie? She's eight now." Pip didn't look comfortable talking about her and changed the subject. "Can I get you a drink?"

"Thanks I'll have a pint of *double diamond* now dad's gone."

"Really? Didn't have you down as a pints sort of girl."

"Danny says I'm better off sticking to beer than start on the shorts. And anyway, I should save something for my eighteenth!"

"Oh so Danny got you drinking, did he?" asked Pip.

"No, I did that all by myself, Danny is my personal advisor and confidante, self appointed but in-valuable nevertheless."

"So, apart from spirit's, what else are you saving until your eighteen?"

"Wouldn't *you* like to know." giggled Nikki.

"Yes, yes I would," he said, quite earnestly and he leant toward her. Nikki didn't get the chance to answer.

"Come and dance with me." yelled Danny.

"Me or him?" shouted Nikki pointing to Pip.

"Both!"

"You go," said Pip "I'll get the beers in."

Chapter Nine

The following afternoon Suzanne and John took Nikki back to the pub to help Bernie and Danny to clear up. It didn't take too long, and within the hour they all sat at the bar.

"What are we all drinking?" offered Danny.

."Orange juice," said Suzanne, "we've got to get back soon. John and Nik have a meeting with the show team."

"Oh yes, quite forgot with all that going on. When's opening night?" asked Danny

"Tuesday and it runs until Saturday. You will try and come along if you can?" asked Nikki.

"I'll try" said Danny. "I love a show."

Nikki arrived at the briefing and was greeted by Tom. He was responsible for the organization of the front of house team and the business management. Tom Denton was twenty two and worked in a bank. Although he didn't exactly sparkle, he was a nice young man, extremely well organized, and despite his age, had a certain amount of authority about him. He showed Nikki the booking sheets he had drawn up to predict ticket sales. He gave the show, exactly the same application he gave to his job. Up until this point, Nikki hadn't realized just how professional the show was. She thought it was an amateur event, put on by a bunch of friends for a laugh and to raise some money. It wasn't. It was an established event, involving large sums of money and was run like a military operation. She began to wonder what she had let herself in for. She needn't have worried. Nikki rose to the challenge, and working closely with Tom, proved to be quite an asset.

Each night after the show the crew and older cast members would go out for a Chinese meal or stay in the theatre bar until the small hours, chatting, singing and relaxing until they were asked to leave.

"Let's have a party after Saturday's final show," said Pip, "I know it's short notice but I bet Nikki can charm her friend Danny to get us the function room again." he put his arm round Nikki's shoulder and winked at her.

"Well, I can ask" smiled Nikki. His tight hug had made her tingle.

"Who's Danny?" Tom asked Nikki "Is he your boyfriend?"

"He's more likely to be *yours*." whooped Pip.

"He's one of my best friends, I work with him."

"Have you got a boyfriend?" continued Tom.

"Not as such." Nikki really didn't want to be having this conversation in front of Pip. She felt awkward. Why she should though, was beyond her.

."Would you go to the party with me, then?"

"We'll all be there together, won't we?"

"Yes I guess we will." Tom sounding deflated.

"Give him a chance Nik, he's trying to ask you out." said Pip with a laugh in his voice.

"I'm well aware of that, I just don't know if I want to go out with him. I haven't known him long."

"What are you waiting for?" asked Pip. Nikki felt herself getting annoyed.

"What's it got to do with *you*?" she snapped. This was quite out of character and it surprised Pip.

"Whoa steady on Nik, I didn't mean anything by it. What's the matter?"

"Nothing, nothing's the matter." This was silly. There *was* something the matter. Pip. She really fancied him. She wanted *him.* What the hell was he doing with Pat, when he could have her? No one understood why they were together. But it was no good. He was out of reach and she was just going to have to deal with that and get any thoughts of being with Pip out of her head. Her infatuation with him was beginning to spoil any chance of a relationship with anyone else.

"I'd better be off." said Nikki "See you all tomorrow. I'll pop and see Danny in the morning and see what we can sort out for Saturday's party. Goodnight all."

Around midday, Nikki *pinged* the reception bell in the *Railway View* Hotel.

"Hello hen, this is an unexpected delight. To what do I owe the pleasure?" grinned Danny.

"I need a favour." said Nikki.

"Oh yeah? Just pop in, use and abuse me - story of my life, - but I wouldn't have thought it of you." Danny leant back his head and putting the back of his hand to his forehead, pretended to look down trodden and bereft. "No hen, really, go on, use and abuse me, brighten my day! It's so dull around here without you this week. What can I do for you? Make it exciting!"

"Firstly, is it time for your break? I thought we could do lunch at the pub."

"Ooh Nicola, are you asking me out? Give me fifteen minutes and I'm all yours. You seem like a girl who enjoys a challenge!" Danny giggled and skipped off to finish his morning jobs.

He and Nikki both had a ploughman's lunch and a pint of lager. Bernie joined them at the table for short while and agreed to the party on Saturday night. Truth be told, he was really pleased to have them in. He knew his takings would benefit greatly. They were nice people, so trouble was unlikely, which was always a bonus. Danny and Nikki started the short walk back to the hotel.

"What's up Nik?" asked Danny, he could sense something was troubling her.

"Nothing. Why?"

"Darling, I know you *too* well. There's something you're not telling your uncle Danny. What is it?"

Nikki felt a little embarrassed. He did know her well, probably better than anyone.

"You'll think I'm stupid. It's nothing really."

"Try me. You'd have to go some for me to think you *stupid* hen."

Nikki told him how she felt about Pip. How he made her feel. How she knew it was silly and that it was getting in the way of her seeing anyone else. Danny was very understanding.

"Damn it, girl, you're in love! And who can blame you - he's gorgeous! But you can't waste your time on him, you're too young. Steer well clear. What he's doing with *her* is beyond me, but he *is* and it ain't gonna change. If he was going to leave her, he would have done it years ago." Danny held the door open and Nikki walked into the hotel reception."

You know that kid ain't *his*?" continued Danny

"Carrie? *Really*? No I didn't" Nikki was surprised. Mainly because she couldn't believe anyone else could fancy Pat.

"Who's is it then?"

"Bugger only knows! I just know it ain't his, he can't have kids."

"Oh. Oh really? Poor Pip."

"That all came out years back when Pat worked here first time around. She used to hang around with a bunch of rough and ready types. The next thing we know she's preggars and she left. She came back a few years later once the sprog started school. In the mean time she married the gorgeous Pip...."

"Why did he stay with her if she had a baby with someone else?"

"Ours not to reason why, hen" said Danny throwing his hands up "But she's got something on him, I don't know what it is. Perhaps he's scared of her? Or what she might do to him if he left. Or what she might do to herself?"

"Like what?"

"Like run under a bus! I don't know Nik, but she's an odd one, we all know that. You'll be wise to stay well away. Now get him out of you mind. It ain't gonna happen. You need a distraction. Leave it to me" said Danny. He was determined to come up with something to help keep his friend away from a situation, which could only end in disaster.

"Love you baby doll" said Danny kissing Nikki on both cheeks "Now run along some of us have work to do."

The after- show party was completely different to Nikki's party the previous week. Sing- songs and dance routines spontaneously erupted throughout the evening amidst an awful lot of drinking. Jo and some of the team from the outdoor activity centre had come down to support the shows last night. Jo was knocking back the drink and had draped herself over Pip. He was obviously enjoying all the attention and was flirting shamelessly with any woman within groping distance. But not Nikki. She thought he was making a fool of himself and she kept her distance. The fact was, she felt extremely jealous but she couldn't allow herself that feeling.

Danny was working the bar with Berni, they made one hell of a double act and amused everyone. Berni announced a lock -in for the regulars using the public bar and everyone partied on until the early hours of the morning. About three o'clock there was still around thirty or so die hards still singing, dancing and drinking, albeit a lot slower. The remaining crowd called it a night around four. Pip had fallen asleep in the corner of the room and Jo was fussing about getting him home. Pat, as usual, had left much earlier in the evening.

"He's alright," said Berni "leave the old sot there, we can chuck him out tomorrow. You can all bunk down here if you like, providing you help me clear up in the morning" Berni fetched a few blankets and many took up the offer. It was beginning to snow outside and the function room was warm, if not a little smelly after the evening revelry. No one noticed, and even if they had, they had drunk far too much to care. Danny and Berni went to the bar to lock up and left them to it to find a suitable place to settle down. Jo snuggled up next to Pip as did three other giggly girls. In the opposite corner eight or nine of the stage crew slept in a heap. Nikki looked round at them all.

"I'm not sleeping in here." she said to Suzanne and John.

"Well I can't drive you home," said John "we've all had too much to drink."

"Don't need you too, I can find my own way. I'm really tired and I want to go home" Nikki had never been the worse for drink before and she wanted the security of her own bed.

"You're not going anywhere *this* time of night." said John suddenly sounding like her teacher again. Nikki wanted to cry.

"Come on hen," said Danny putting his arm round her "you three can have the next room."

.Adjoining the function room was a lounge area, small bathroom, a kitchenette and double bedroom. Danny had often stayed there and tonight he and Berni were using the double bedroom. The lounge sofa was a lot more comfortable that the dance floor and Nikki soon settled down to sleep with Suzanne and John close by on the carpeted floor.

It seemed no time at all before the radio and the smell of bacon woke Nikki. It was nine thirty. John and Suzanne were up and Berni and Danny had already left the flat. They had left a clean towel out for Nikki with an oversized tee-shirt which belonged to Danny for her to change into if she wanted to. This was accompanied by a note:

Hope you slept ok, I had to go to work. Help yourself to brekkie. Have a good day, meet me in the bar this evening, I've got a surprise for you. Love you D ☺ *xx Ps. It might cheer you to know, Pip puked all over that tart that slept on him! – ha ha.*

Ha, thought Nikki. It did cheer her. Jo was all over Pip last night it served her right.

Nikki couldn't bring herself to eat anything. She washed briefly and changed into the tee shirt. By the time she went through to the function room, most of the clearing up was done. Only Suzanne John and Tom remained.

"We're pretty much finished here now." said John "I'm starving"

"Danny's left bacon and stuff out for us. I could make some bacon butties if you like." said Nikki, praying he'd say no, as the thought of cooking made her feel even worse than she already did.

"Let's just go home," said Suzanne "I feel dirty and I want to shower. I'm knackered, John, and I've got a lot on this week."

"Sorry, darling." said John "You've done more than your fair share this week helping us out, thank you."

"I don't mind, you know that, but I've had enough now." Suzanne looked exhausted.

"I'd like breakfast with you." said Tom

"Some other time." said Nikki

"Really? When?"

"Maybe not." laughed Nikki "I just meant not now. Time we got going."

"Can I see you later?" asked Tom.

"Sorry, I'm seeing Danny tonight."

"What is it with you two? You do know he's a poof?" Tom was annoyed.

"I don't care what you or anyone else thinks he is, he's my best friend and you can keep your opinions to yourself. He asked to see me tonight and I want to. Even if I didn't, after all he's done for us over the last few days, I think I owe him that, don't you?"

Tom persisted "Can I see you in the week then?"

"I don't know what I'm doing yet." Nikki really wasn't that interested in Tom and he was beginning to annoy her.

"I'll call you then?"

"If you want to. Bye Tom." Nikki opened the car door and sat down behind her sister.

"He really likes you Nik, why were you so unkind?" Suzanne asked her.

"I know he does, he's just a bit pushy."

"You do like him though?" asked John as he started the engine.

"He's ok."

"Perhaps the four of us could go out together sometime?" suggested John

"Good grief, are you trying to fix me up again? You know what happened last time with Mick?"

"No, I just promised him I'd put in a word for him, that's all, you can't blame the boy for trying."

The three of them arrived home just in time for one of Marion's Sunday roasts.

"Dinner's about ready to be dished up. Have you all had a good time?" asked Marion "You look worn out, all of you."

"It was great fun – tiring - but great fun. Dinner looks

great, Marion, thank you so much, we're ready for this." said John.

Sunday afternoon in the Edward's house was very quiet. The end of the show had left John and Nikki feeling a little deflated. Suzanne had been helping out all week, one way or another, mainly ironing the cast's costumes, which is a constantly necessary, yet forever thankless, task. She, Nikki and John all succumbed to sleep as they sat in the cosy front room by the roaring fire. Derek was reading the papers and Marion sat quietly darning a patch in the elbow of his favourite green cardigan which had seen much better days. Marion smiled at her family. She counted her blessings. John was the first to open his eyes.

"Oooh, sorry Marion. I must have dosed off. Must have been that wonderful lunch." he said feeling a little embarrassed.

"It's flattering you feel that comfortable." smiled Marion. She really liked John. She hoped, one day, he would become her son-in-law.

"What are your plans for the rest of the day?" she asked.

"A quiet night in, I think. School breaks up at the end of this week. There's quite a lot to finish off. I need to be up early tomorrow."

The conversation woke the two girls.

"What about you Nikki? Are you back to work tomorrow? asked her mother.

"I'm on lates' this week," said Nikki rubbing her eyes "Wow, look at the time, I'm meeting Danny in half an hour."

"You're never at home these days." chipped in Derek without looking up from the paper.

"Dad, I had every evening at home for years, I want to go out"

"Where are you going?"

"Just to the Loco, Danny's got a surprise for me."

"Like what?"

"Dunno Dad, it's a surprise." Nikki got up, kissed her father on the top of his head and went off to get showered and changed.

Danny was waiting by the bar, with a tall dark haired man in his mid twenties.

"Now, here she is," squealed Danny "looking an awful lot better than when I last saw her, thank God." He jumped off the bar stool and hugged her. "This my lovie, is my surprise. Meet Raymond."

"Hi".

He had a deep, smooth voice. The sort of voice that gets a bloke noticed.

"Call me Ray," he smiled. "Danny was right."

"Right? Right about what?" asked Nikki

"He said you were cute."

"Cute?" questioned Nikki looking at Danny.

"Well, she has her moments." said Danny "Perhaps I should have said feisty?"

"Perhaps you shouldn't have said anything at all? I'm Nikki" she added, "you can choose your own adjective, once Danny's got us all a drink."

"I'll get them Danny, what would you like Nikki?"

"Just a coke please."

"Well, you kept him quiet." Nikki said as she turned to Danny "Doesn't Berni mind you bringing him in here?"

"Why should he?"

"I just thought…"

"Ooh no, he's not with me, he's for you hen."

"What?"

"I told you I had a surprise for *you.* Ray's *your* surprise. He saw you at the hotel a couple of weeks ago and asked for your number. You know I'd never give that out. I told him, if he wanted it, he'd have to ask for it himself. So he asked me to fix it up. What'd you think?"

"I think he's lovely Danny, but you could have warned me"

"Why? You would have told me not to interfere and probably wouldn't have come."

"Shall we get a table?" interrupted Ray.

"Thank you." said Nikki taking her drink and followed Ray to the table. Danny didn't join them, he winked at Nikki and went behind the bar to give Berni a hand.

"So tell me all about yourself." said Ray "All I know is your name, you work at the *Railway View,* until you decide what you want to do with your life, and you have a friend called Danny, who adores you and is very protective."

Nikki laughed. "That's about it, not much else to tell."

"I'm sure that's not true. What did you do last summer?" Ray was charming. He was so easy to talk to. He was funny and interesting, attentive and extremely attractive. They talked for a couple of hours and Ray told her he lived in London but would be staying at the hotel for the first few months of the new year, as the company he worked for had a number of projects in the region.

"Can we meet up again on Thursday?" he asked as Nikki got up to leave.

"I'd like that, but I'm working until nine." she replied

"Perfect, we'll have a late dinner" he smiled. Nikki liked his confidence and the way he took control.

"Can I give you a lift home?"

"Thank you. That'll be nice. I was going to walk, but it's a lot colder than I expected. Good night Danny, see you tomorrow." called Nikki as she left with Ray.

"Goodnight, sweet pea. Be good." Danny called back.

Rays Capri, pulled up outside the house just as John was saying goodnight to Suzanne.

"Who's that?" asked Ray.

"My sister Suze and her bloke John. I'll get the third degree now they've seen you." she laughed.

"Then let's give them something to interrogate you about." he said and took Nikki face in his hands and kissed her lips. Nikki felt herself go weak.

"Okay?" asked Ray softly.

"Okay." smiled Nikki.

"Thursday then?" asked Ray "I'll meet you in reception when you finish."

"Better not." said Nikki.

"Why? I'm sorry I thought you wanted to?"

"Oh I do, I meant better not meet in reception. We're not supposed to fraternise with the guests"

"Are you going to fraternise with me then? I thought we were having dinner?"

Nikki felt herself blush. "You know what I mean" she said.

"Fair enough. Here's the challenge then. I'll order dinner for my room and you get yourself in without being seen. Do you think you could do that?"

"I'm sure Danny will help."

"Thursday then, nine o'clock."

"Nine o'clock." repeated Nikki

"I'll look forward to it".

"Me too." said Nikki as Ray leaned towards her to say goodnight and this time the kiss lingered.

Chapter Ten

All day Thursday Nikki felt excited. So did Danny, come to that. They devised a plan to get Nikki into Ray's room, which involved Danny being responsible for delivering dinner.

What a farce that was! It was a good thing that Nikki was small, otherwise she would never have been able to have squeezed herself into the bottom of the trolley. Danny hung a large cloth over it, and her, and made his way along the corridor towards Ray's room.

"Just be quiet hen or we'll *both* be in trouble." Danny instructed with more than a hint of worry in his voice. Nikki was finding it very difficult not to laugh.

"Room service" Danny called as he knocked the door.

"Hi Danny, is everything okay? Have you seen Nikki? Ray asked.

Danny pushed the trolley into Ray's room in a very obvious cloak and dagger way.

"She's down there." he mouthed, pulling a face that resembled a character of Les Dawson and pointed to the base of the trolley. Ray lifted the cloth.

"Good evening Nikki, are you okay?" he giggled. Nikki felt silly.

"Not the greatest ride I've ever had." she said as she tried to climb out with some sort of dignity. "The night is yet young!" smirked Danny as he winked at Ray and turned to leave the room. "Enjoy!" he called to Ray and then moved in to whisper to Nikki.

"I've called your dad Nik, told him we're short staffed and we're all staying on to muck in. So you've got all night, if you want it, fill your boots, hen!" Danny kissed Nikki on the cheek and continued, "If you need me, call room service, me, I'll rescue you." Danny was so sweet. He loved the excitement of it all, but more importantly was genuinely making sure his friend was alright.

"Champagne?" Ray poured out two tall glasses as Danny closed the door and left them alone together.

"Lovely thank you." smiled Nikki. She didn't know if it was lovely or not. She had never tasted real champagne before and it went straight to her head. That coupled with the fact she really fancied Ray made it easy for her to relax with him. They enjoyed the supper Danny had delivered and chatted about nothing and everything. Nikki felt she had known Ray a lot longer than a couple of days. He was interesting and so easy going. They finished the meal and snuggled up together on the large soft sofa, listening to music and finishing off the bottle.

"Shall I order another?" asked Ray. Nikki loved the champagne but was already feeling a little more tipsy, than she would have liked.

"No I'm fine thank you."

"Can I get you anything else?"

"No, I'm fine thank you." said Nikki repeating herself.

"Don't be nervous, Nikki, you don't have to do anything you don't want to." whispered Ray as he gently started to kiss her neck. His lips were warm and soft and the way he kissed her made her feel completely at his mercy. He slid his hand up inside her blouse and could feel her nipples harden. She knew she wanted him. She pulled away slightly and started to unbutton her clothing. Ray smiled.

"You're beautiful Nikki" he said and pulled his shirt off over his head.

Wow! thought Nikki. He was tanned and muscular with thick chest hair that she wanted to lose herself in. they went over to the bed, undressed to the waist. The room was dimly lit, only the bedside light remained on. Nikki wanted Ray so much. She lay down beside him and he moved down her body to remove the rest of her clothes. He held her close to him as he caressed her young skin.

"You are sure you're okay about this?" he gently asked her again.

"I don't think I've ever wanted anything more before in my life." she said softly.

"You tell me if you want me to stop." he said. She could feel how hard he was and longed for it. "I will." she said as he gently turned her onto her back. Ray kissed her breasts as he put his hand between her legs. "Oh darling, that's lovely."

"I want you, Ray."

"You've got me, sweetheart." he said as he slid up, deep inside her.

For the next two weeks, Ray and Nikki spent as much time as they could together. He wasn't at the hotel every night and sometimes he would be away for a couple of days, but they took every opportunity they could to make love and Nikki thought it was wonderful. Ray had to go back to London over Christmas to be with family and to prepare for the weeks he would be working away in the New Year. So, on the Friday before Christmas, he asked to take Nikki out for a meal.

"I'll pick you up." he said. Nikki's parents had only half an idea that their daughter had a new boyfriend and hadn't really asked too many questions. All they had heard was from Suzanne that a good looking bloke in a Ford Capri had dropped Nikki home a couple of weeks ago and she saw him kiss her goodnight.

"So, where are you off to this evening?" Marion asked as Nikki came down the stairs "You look lovely."

"Good grief, he must be special, our Nikki's got a dress on!" laughed Derek. Nikki only owned one dress; she rarely wore it as she felt self conscious about the scarring on her legs. It didn't matter with Ray; he'd seen them, he'd seen everything! It hadn't made any difference to him and this had been a massive confidence boost to her.

"We're going to the *Ancient Swan*." replied Nikki.

"Blimey, get you," joked Derek "you got yourself a millionaire then?" The *Ancient Swan* was a very expensive restaurant and the Edward's had never eaten there. There was a knock at the front door. Derek got up to answer it and returned to the sitting room with Ray in tow.

"Good evening, Mrs Edwards." said Ray "Thank you for allowing me to take your beautiful daughter to dinner, these are for you." he said as he handed her a box of luxury chocolates.

"Oh thank you, how kind." said Marion "Nikki says you're going to the *Ancient Swan*, how lovely."

"Only the best for Nikki."

"Well, have a lovely evening you two."

"Thank you, we will" said Ray.

"Thanks mum, don't wait up." said Nikki and she left holding the hand of the extremely dashing and smartly dressed Ray.

"What a lovely man." said Marion.

"Bit old for our Nikki isn't he? And why's he creeping round you with chocolates?" grunted Derek.

"It's called good manners." said Marion.

"Well I'm not so sure about him, seems a bit smarmy to me." said Derek and went back to watching the television.

The following Monday was Christmas Eve. A huge, beautiful and very expensive bouquet of flowers was delivered to the Edwards house. The card read: *Merry Christmas, darling. Ray* xx

"He must think an awful lot of her." said Marion as she took delivery of them.

"All a bit over the top isn't it?" replied Derek. There was something about Ray that didn't sit right with Derek. He didn't know what it was, but there was something. Marion thought he was lovely and that Derek was just too protective of his youngest daughter.

Christmas came and went without much incident. Suzanne and John divided the holiday between both their families. Derek had allowed John to stay over on Christmas day night, but on a made up bed in the back room, not with Suzanne. The girls would laugh sometimes about their parent's old fashioned ways but respected them and wouldn't think of acting against them. Not if they thought they might be found out anyway. Nikki knew if her father was aware of her true relationship with Ray, Christmas would not have been a happy one at all.

The hotel was hosting a New Years Eve event and consequently, it was all hands to the pumps. Nikki found herself working all hours as she had promised Mrs Pyke when she had been granted holiday earlier in December. She really didn't mind. Ray was away and the work was a distraction. She missed him. The atmosphere at the hotel was happy and festive. The guests, some of which stayed every Christmas and New Year just for the company, were all in good spirits and extremely generous with their tips. It was four am before Danny and Nikki were able to clear away the last of the buffet and start to tidy the reception ready for the morning.

"When's Ray due back?" Danny asked, "I can see you've missed him."

"Not until the fourteenth."

"How's it going? Is he still making you happy?"

"Yeah it's good, I'm happy, he's great." she smiled

"I bet he is! Lucky you. Tell me all the juicy bits."

"No way!" she laughed "But they *are* juicy."

They both laughed.

"I'm so glad you've got someone nice."

"Well he's not really mine, is he?" said Nikki

"Blimey, you wouldn't be wanting to get engaged or something, already would you?"

"No, I mean he's not *mine*, he's someone else's." Danny looked confused. "Do I have to spell it out Danny? Ray's married. I thought you knew that. Why do you think he's gone home for Christmas?"

"Oh my God Nikki. No, I didn't know. What do you take me for? Oh my God, what have I done?" Danny was distraught. He held his hands up to his face and squeezed his cheeks together.

Nikki stopped polishing the reception desk. She walked round behind the desk to stand beside her friend.

"You haven't done anything wrong Danny"

"But I *have*. I introduced you, fixed you up, smuggled you into his room. Need I go on?"

"No, I wish you wouldn't. I'm glad you fixed us up. He's gorgeous and you said yourself I had to lose it sometime to someone. I'm glad it was him. Ray's been brilliant. He was honest with me from the start. It was *my* choice. I thought, why not?"

"Nicola Edwards, you never cease to amaze me. I don't know what you were thinking. I can't believe it. Oh God, Nik what a *mess*. You don't love him do you?"

"No Danny, I don't. He spoils me, treats me nice, we have fantastic sex and that's it, no strings" "But he's met your parents. What do they say about it all?"

"Ah well yes, that *is* a bit of a problem. It made it easier not to keep him a secret. I didn't really plan on mum liking him so much."

"I take it they don't know then?"

"Hell no! They'd *kill* me. Look, Danny, it's no big deal. He's only here for a few months and then that's it, we'll both move on. No harm done."

"And you'll just be able to do that will you? Danny was concerned it could all turn nasty. He thought Nikki was falling for him and could see this wouldn't be as easy for her to end it and she might think.

"I don't love him Danny, I *lust* him, BIG difference."

"We'll see." said Danny, unconvinced. He looked down at the signing in book pretending to read it. Nikki picked up the duster and put it back into the cleaning holdall.

"In the mean time, stop worrying about me. I consider myself available and am still on the lookout for Mr Right."

"Oooh you hussy! Where did my shy little naive Nicola go?" questioned Danny

"She went to the *Railway View* hotel, met the outgoing, outlandish and outrageous little Danny who lead her astray and she loves him for it! Please stop worrying." She said as he squeezed his hand gently, before heading toward the stair case.

Danny smiled at her, but was deeply regretful of the whole situation. He may have been outrageous, but he had standards.

Ray returned on the fourteenth as promised. Nikki was behind reception as he came over to check himself back in. She wanted to hug him but instead she smiled professionally and welcomed the returning guest back. He waited until it was just the two of them at the desk.

"This is for you." he said as he pulled a small beautifully wrapped gift box out of his pocket. "Happy new year darling. Sorry they're a bit late." he said.

"Wow they're lovely." she said looking at the diamond stud earrings "They must have cost a fortune."

"You're worth it. Did you miss me?"

"Yes of *course* I did. Thank you Ray, they're beautiful."

"Wear them tonight." he said.

"Where are we going?"

"Room forty four, wear them and nothing else." Ray gave Nikki a cheeky grin and winked as he went up to his room.

That evening she did exactly as he had requested and showed him just how much she had missed him.

On Friday evening John and Suzanne came to pick Nikki up from work. They were all going into town to meet up with some of the show crew for drinks. Nikki was making up an extra bed in one of the guest rooms when they arrived, so they waited for her in reception. Danny came over to wish them a happy new year.

"You too" replied Suzanne and stood up to kiss his cheek.

"So what are we going to do about our naughty Nikki then?"

"Why? What's she done now? laughed John.

"You know, I just don't want her getting hurt that's all" said Danny

"Neither do we Danny, do you think she will then? She seems to be getting on very well with Ray"

"Yes she is. *Very* well. That's what worries me. Not the best situation is it? With him being married?" Danny could see by the look on their faces that he had put his foot in it.

"He's *what*!? shouted Suzanne.

"Oh God. Me and my big mouth. I thought you knew."

"No I didn't" puffed Suzanne. Just at that minute Nikki came down the stairs.

"Hi everyone, I won't be a minute."

She saw the look on Suzanne's face "What's the matter Suze?"

"Is Ray married?" Suzanne glared at her little sister with an expression of both disgust and disappointment.

"Danny!" snapped Nikki.

"Sorry, hen, I thought you would have told your sister," He turned and shrugged at Suzanne and trying to defend himself. "I only found out myself a couple of days ago."

"What the *hell* do you think you're doing? Dad's going to kill you!"

"You're not going to *tell* him are you?" begged Nikki "*Please* Suze, he doesn't need to know. Ray's only here for a few months. We're just having a bit of fun, no one need get hurt."

"No way Nik! Listen to yourself. I'm telling Dad. It's about time you grew up and took a bit of responsibility."

"Whoa hang on there, Suze. You're no saint. I wasn't the one sleeping with a teacher before I left school." snapped Nikki

. "Neither was I!"

"Prove it," Nikki stared at John.

"Leave it Suze. Nikki's right, there's no point in upsetting your Mum and Dad." said John "Thanks John." said Nikki, relieved.

"I'm not doing it for *you* Nik, I don't want your parents upset. You make sure this ends right now."

"You can't tell me what to do anymore John. I'm not at school now."

"Then stop behaving like a stupid kid, I'm trying to *help* you."

"Leave me alone, *all* of you! It's none of your business."

Nikki went off to the staff rest room. She was furious with Suzanne and John and even more so with Danny. Danny appeared at the door.

"They've left without you" he said sheepishly.

"Good. I don't want anything to do with any of them right this moment."

"I'm sorry hen. What are you going to do?" asked Danny.

"Right now? I'm going home before you and me fall out big time. She got up and headed for the door. "Night, Danny." And she left, to walk home alone.

Ray was back at the hotel Monday morning. Nikki had used the weekend to decide what she should do. Now Suzanne and John knew, she felt guilty about her relationship with Ray and decided she would have to tell him it was finished, for everyone's sake. She saw him go up to his room and followed a few minutes later.

"Hi Nikki, this is a nice welcome, I've literally only just got here." smiled Ray.

"I know, I was waiting for you. There's something you need to know."

"What's up Nik?"

"Suzanne and John know you're married. So does Danny come to that. Suzes is going to tell my parents if I don't stop seeing you."

"Oh I see, is that it then? Don't you want to see me anymore?"

"Yes of *course* I do. But it would be the right thing to do, wouldn't it? We both knew it was only for a while anyway, didn't we?......... and if you don't soon take that shirt off I think I may have to rip it off....." Nikki pushed him backward on to the bed.

"Of course we'll stop it but I can't, not just yet." she said.

The sex was urgent and passionate and brief but made her feel happier.

"See you tonight." said Nikki as she left his room. Ray smiled to himself, he felt like he'd been hit by a whirlwind. Nikki was exciting.

Nikki felt bad lying to her sister but it wouldn't be for long. She felt worse lying to Danny. She was sure he knew but if he did, he didn't let on.

"Suzanne tells me you've broken up with Ray," said Marion during dinner later that week "I'm sorry, he was a nice young man. You don't seem too upset, what went wrong?"

"Nothing mum, he just wasn't right for me. That's all."

"I didn't like him." said Derek "Bit of a flash Harry if you want my opinion, you'd be better off finding someone your own age."

"Thanks Dad, but I'm really not that interested at the moment."

"So, have you decided what it is you want to do yet?" asked Derek.

"About what?"

"Your career. You said that hotel was a brief stop gap while you decide what it is you want to do."

"I like it there."

"If she's happy that's fine for now, isn't it? chipped in Marion.

"No I haven't yet, Dad, but at least I'm happy and in work *while* I'm deciding"

"Just don't waste your life, Nikki. Promise me you'll give it some serious thought? You'll be surprised just how quickly time goes. Before you know it you've lost ten years and you won't know where they've gone."

Nikki kissed the top of Derek's head.

"You worry too much, Dad. I promise to give it some thought." Nikki didn't want to leave anything just yet. Not her job, not her friend Danny and *definitely* not Ray.

Chapter Eleven

By the time the summer came Ray had gone back to London. Although they were sad to part, neither regretted the relationship and they both had wonderful memories. Nikki had been on a couple of dates but nothing worth mentioning and was now dating a barman from the *Locomotive* called Howard. He was a nice lad of twenty-one and although Nikki found him a bit childish at times they had a good laugh together. Nikki liked him, but he felt like a little brother to her. He was quite *needy,* but in a way, she quite liked that. She hadn't really felt needed by anyone before. They saw each other most evenings spent all their free time together. He had made it easier for her to get over Ray leaving. Although they were, to all intents and purposes, a couple, they were no more intimate than a kiss and cuddle. Nikki wasn't ready for another serious relationship yet and anyway, she couldn't imagine being with Howard like that. Howard, on the other hand, was besotted with Nikki and at times she felt this rather stifling. They had been *going steady* as Marion put it, for a couple months when quite out of the blue Howard proposed, just three weeks before Nikki's eighteenth birthday.

"Oh for God's sake, get up," said Nikki "What the hell are you doing?"

Howard was on bended knee in the Locomotive pub, surrounded by the locals.

"I'm asking you to marry me Nikki, I love you and I want you to be my wife." Everyone cheered.

"I'm *seventeen*," said Nikki "I'm nowhere near ready to settle down yet, I want to live a little first and get a career."

"You won't *need* a career, you and me can have our own pub," grinned Howard. "It'll be great." "No it won't. I don't want to smell of beer and cigarette smoke all my life, I want to make something of myself; see the world a bit. *Please* get up."

Howard grabbed her hands, "No," he said trying not to look hurt "you want to be with me, we're meant to be together, if you don't marry me, I'll kill myself."

"Oh don't be such a drama queen. We're way too young. I don't want to marry you Howard. I don't want to marry anyone. *Please* get up you're making a scene." The pub went quiet. Howard stood up and left the bar.

Nikki was left feeling awkward as everyone looked at her for some sort of reaction.

"What? I had no idea he was going to do that. We've only been going out a few weeks. I haven't done anything wrong. Stop looking at me like that."

"Someone better go after him." said Berni.

Nikki sighed, "I'll go. See if I can talk some sense into him."

Nikki stepped outside. The night air had turned very

cold and the slush on the steps had started to freeze over. She pulled the suede collar of her coat up around her ears and looked for Howard. She could see him walking quickly away on the other side of the road. She started down the steps to go after him.

As she did so, she slipped. Falling to the ground she felt a familiar tear in her leg. Oh no, not now. She thought that was all behind her. She couldn't get up. Her leg was twisted and locked, bent at the knee. She was in agony. Luckily Suzanne and John had just pulled up at the pub and had witnessed her fall. They rushed to her aid. Carefully they lifted her into John's car and took her to hospital.

Nikki underwent surgery the following day.

Her family were standing around the bed when her surgeon, Mr Monkford, came to explain the situation. Nikki was in traction and a great deal of discomfort.

"The good news is you should be home in time for Christmas. The bad news is you'll be spending your eighteenth birthday in here." he smiled kindly at her but Nikki felt awful. The last thing on her mind was her birthday or Christmas, come to that.

"Well, she had a lovely party last year, didn't you love?" said Marion trying to lighten the mood. "I'll see you tomorrow," said the doctor, "Get some rest young lady. Please don't stay too long, she needs her sleep."

"We'll be off in a minute" replied John

"We can pop in the Loco and let everyone know what's happened." said Suzanne.

"I'd really rather you didn't." said Nikki.

"They'll have to be told something. Howard will wonder where you are."

"Oh my God, Howard." exclaimed Nikki sitting up and jolting her leg "Arrrrahh!"

"What's the matter?" asked Suzanne.

"He asked me to marry him last night, that's why I rushed out the pub after him. He said he was going to kill himself."

"I hope you turned him down." said Derek.

"Yes, obviously Dad, that's was why he was going to kill himself."

"Oh I wasn't sure, thought it was because you'd said yes." laughed Derek.

"This isn't funny, he was really upset. I'm worried about him Suze."

"Don't be, we'll find him. You've got enough on your plate right now." said John, "We'll pop back again tomorrow and put your mind at rest."

He patted Nikki hand. Suzanne hugged her sister.

"You don't deserve this, Nik. Hope you can sleep alright, see you tomorrow."

"Just make sure he's okay."

"What shall we tell him?"

"Well, I don't want him here," said Nikki "I don't want to see him anymore at all. He was so intense! But please let him down gently."

"Okay. Goodnight Nik."

When Suzanne returned the next day she told Nikki that she had seen Howard. She sat down by Nikki's bed. She looked really worried and Nikki instantly knew something was wrong.

"Whatever's happened Suze?

"It's Howard. He's in the hospital, Nik. He stabbed himself."

"Oh *shit*. Is it bad? This is all *my* fault."

"No, it isn't bad, and no, it isn't your fault. You mustn't blame yourself. Apparently he's done something like this before with a previous girlfriend. You're well shot of him, who knows what he might do next?" Suzanne's worried look turned to a smile "Bloody hell Nik, you do pick 'em!"

"He is going to be alright though, isn't he?"

"Yeah he'll be fine. He slashed his upper arm. Attention seeking if you ask me. I mean, if you *really* intend to kill yourself, you'd go for the wrist or your heart of something major wouldn't you? I think he wanted you to feel sorry for him and agree to marry him. Bit sad really."

Suzanne sat on the bed beside her sister. They shared the thin grey plastic headphones to listen to the chart show on Radio 1. They always listened to this together although their taste in music was very different. Suzanne loved the Osmond's. Nikki found *them* a bit soppy. She was a big fan of Slade, Suzi Quartro, and more recently Queen. Anything loud really. The girls bedroom wall posters were strikingly different.

It wasn't long before John arrived to collect Suzanne.

"Time we left her in peace, I think." he said, softly "You look tired Nik. Try and get some sleep."

"Did you tell everyone?"

"Only some of the crew, Mick & Rosie send their love. Tom wants to visit. I said I'd have to ask first."

"Yeah, he'll be someone different to talk to, break up the day a bit. Thanks John. Thank you both for everything."

They said their goodbyes. Nikki watched them leave.

The main ward lights were off as soon as the last visitors left. Only her dim bed side light remained on. The five other women in the ward, were all elderly and had long since gone to sleep. Nikki sunk back in the pillows. Her leg was painful and she was *very* uncomfortable. The auxiliary nurse pushed the hot drinks trolley round to the side f Nikki's bed.

"Quiet in here" she smiled and poured Nikki her usual hot chocolate. The hospital hot-chocolate was by far, the highlight of all the food and drink served. Nikki looked forward to it.

She sipped her drink and thought about Howard. She felt sorry for him. It was sad, but she wouldn't be with someone out of pity. She thought about the year she had just had. An awful lot had happened to her. Most of it good. She thought about Ray, with fondness. She had missed him but had always known the affair was just that, an affair, nothing more. She thought about how that had caused her to lie to her parents. This, she was deeply sorry for. It saddened her, they didn't deserve that and she felt ashamed. She thought about missing her eighteenth birthday celebrations and being out of action for Christmas. All these thoughts swirled round and round in her head. She realized that more than anything at this moment in time, what she felt most, was sorry for *herself*. She turned her head to one side, pressed it into the pillow and in the darkness, she sobbed.......

"Nikki" the gentle voice whispered close to her ear. "Is this a bad time?" The kind voice was soft and familiar. And one she hadn't heard in over a year.

It was Pip.

"No. It's fine. What are you doing here?" The mixed emotions whipped through her like a hurricane.

"I brought some show tickets up for the nursing staff who support us. So, I thought I'd pop in and see how you are."

"It's late. How did you get in? They're really strict. They don't let anyone in after visiting time."

"Nikki. How do you think? I smiled! How could they resist me?" The fact was, this was probably true. He had that way about him. "I was rather hoping you'd be helping us out again this year but I guess that's out of the question now."

"I'm really sorry, I'd love to...... I've let everyone down." Nikki felt the tears fall from her eyes. Pip took out his handkerchief and gently wiped her cheek.

"Not at all, but we will miss you. I was beginning to think you were avoiding me."

"No, I'm not. Why would you....?"

"I'm teasing Nik. Listen, get well very soon, I'd better go before they chuck me out I was only allowed a couple of minutes. I just wanted to see how you were doing and to let you know we were all thinking of you." Pip bent over the bed and gently kissed her forehead.

"Get well soon sweetheart, and Happy Birthday for next week."

Nikki smiled. Pip always made things seem better.

"Thank you. Good luck with the show. Or should I say break a leg?" Pip took her hand, it made her feel warm inside.

"Look after yourself. I'll keep tabs on your progress via John, and, when you're back on your feet, we'll celebrate your birthday properly, how does that sound?" He looked deep into her eyes as he said goodbye. She was sure he knew how she felt about him, but neither of them had ever said anything. Why did she feel like that? Nothing had ever happened between them. Keeping away from him for the past year had made no difference. Even though she was in pain and at her lowest point, he still made her feel better. Her heart skipped a beat when she saw him. What was it about him? She was old enough to know that what she felt was love. She didn't know why but from the moment she had first seen him, something happened, something she couldn't explain, something no one can explain. Silly really. But it still happens and there is nothing you can do about it.

Thinking of Pip helped Nikki sleep a lot better that night.

Chapter Twelve

"Hi, how are you today? John said it would be alright to visit, is it okay?" blurted Tom the following afternoon.

"Yes its fine, Tom, hello."

"I wasn't sure, I didn't know if you'd mind really, I didn't know if you'd have lots of visitors. Wow that's some contraption" Tom indicated to the traction and the pins through her knee "Does it hurt? I bet it hurts like hell, I broke my toe once."

"For God's sake, Tom, take a breath will you?"

"Sorry, I don't like hospitals much, they make me nervous."

"I don't like them either funnily enough, but I'm stuck here."

"Sorry. I thought after all the years you've been in and out of them you'd be used to it by now." "No, just more pissed off every time! If you've come to cheer me up you need to change the subject" Nikki was annoyed. Tom seemed to know about her past and she would be having words with John and Suzanne later.

The physiotherapist came on to the ward.

"I'd better go," said Tom "Sorry, I'll see you tomorrow." He stopped as he reached the door, turned round and came back and put the flowers he had brought her on the bed.

"These are for you." he said as he practically ran for the door again.

The physiotherapist arrived, just as Tom was rushing out. Christine had worked at the hospital for the past ten years and had been assigned to Nikki in the past. They had got to know each other quite well over the years and Nikki liked her. She was firm but fair and worked Nikki hard, knowing from her own experience what Nikki was going through.

"Is that your young man?" she asked.

"No, he's just a friend. I think I make him nervous."

"I think that's because he likes you."

"Maybe, or it might be because he doesn't like hospitals. I'm not really sure why he came. Perhaps I'll find out tomorrow if he's brave enough to come back" The two girls giggled.

"You may not be quite as scary tomorrow, it looks like we may be able to remove some of the scaffolding later today" said Christine.

"Oh great joy, my bums getting really sore stuck in the same position."

It was the following morning that Nikki was taken down to the minor surgery unit to have the pins disconnected from the side of her knee. This meant that she was no longer physically attached to the structure that prevented her from getting out of bed. She also had the plaster cast removed so she was able to scratch her leg – bliss! She was then wheeled off to see Martin, the plaster man, who was to re-set her leg from hip to ankle. Martin and Nikki were on first name terms. He had started his apprenticeship in the orthopaedic department when Nikki was first a patient there nine years earlier. It was on her that Martin had first set a plaster on a *real* patient. He had even made her a mock certificate to commemorate it. He was kind and funny and had set her leg more than thirty times over the years. By the time her parents visited that evening, Nikki felt much brighter. She was sitting up with her new dazzling white plaster supported by pillows.

"Oh that's better." said Marion kissing her daughter. "You must be so much more comfortable."

"I am. They are planning to get me up and about tomorrow. I can't wait, if only to use a proper toilet!"

"Don't try and do too much too soon." said Derek.

"I'm not Dad, I'm just doing what I'm told. I should be home for Christmas."

"You've got your birthday first."

Her birthday was the following day but for all she cared it could have been months away.

"Well it's not going to be much of one is it, stuck in here?" said Nikki, beginning to feel down again. Sometimes Derek had the most annoying way of stating the obvious, whether you needed reminding of it or not.

"Never mind sweetheart," said Marion "let's concentrate on getting you well and home for Christmas. We can have a late birthday in the new year."

"Thanks mum, I'd like that."

After a while Marion got up to leave. She had a pile of Christmas cards she wanted to deliver on the way home.

"Well, we'd better be off, everyone wants to see you

tomorrow, I don't suppose there's anyone else to come tonight, get some rest." she said as she kissed her daughter goodbye.

Nikki settled back in her bed. She was glad that tomorrow at least she would be getting up, but try as she might she couldn't help feeling sorry for herself. Just before nine, as she was settling down to sleep, Tom came rushing in.

"I can't come tomorrow, I'm glad really, because I didn't want to give you a present in front of everyone. Ooh, you look a lot better. I'm glad that pin things gone, that looked dreadful. Are you feeling better? I hope so..."

"Hello Tom. Have you got me a present then?" Tom handed her an oblong box. Inside was a silver engraved pen.

"Thank you, Tom, that's really kind of you."

"I've got to go, they say I can only be here until nine else they will lock me in."

She was sure Tom thought this would actually happen. He wasn't taking any chances. He lent forward to kiss her cheek as he wished her Happy Birthday, and as he did so he knocked the water jug flying.

"Oh God, I'm so sorry." Tom was bumbling and flustered.

"It's okay Tom. You'd better go, see you soon?"

"I'd like that. Can I come and see you at home before Christmas?"

"Yes please do"

He leant forward again for a second attempt to kiss her. This time, his foot slipped on the wet floor and sat down in rather a hurry. With the seat of his trousers soaked through and looking rather embarrassed, Tom left the ward.

Nikki was able to leave the hospital on the sixteenth of

December and by Christmas Eve, Tom had visited more than eight times. He put in some long hours at the bank but if he said he was going to see her, he did. Making money was high on his agenda, not something Nikki's family was particularly familiar with, it wasn't the be- all-and-end-all, but as Derek said, that wasn't always a bad thing. He fitted in with the Edwards family pretty well and it wasn't long before he and Nikki began to see each other in a more romantic light.

It was early spring before she was able to return to work full time. She had done a few shifts to ease herself in gently, mostly working reception but wasn't able to return full time until she could walk completely unaided again. It was then she also felt ready to make up for missing her eighteenth birthday.

"We could all go out for a meal." suggested Tom.

"Nice." she said sarcastically "It's my eighteenth Tom, we could do that anytime."

"A party then?"

"Let's all have a weekend away?" said Suzanne "We haven't done that for ages."

"Just the four of us? We'd better not go too far; Nikki will have to be careful" Tom said looking worried.

"Or we could see if any of the crowd want to tag along. It's up to Nik. It's her party"

"I don't care who comes. I'm just looking forward to getting away!" beamed Nikki.

"I could see if the activity centre's available?" suggested John.

"That'll be great. Let's plan for May bank holiday" Nikki really began to feel like her old self again now she had this to look forward to. Tom went along with it although he wasn't at all sure she was up to it.

John organised everything and when the Friday of May bank holiday arrived, he, Suzanne, Nikki, Tom, Mick, Rosie, Lynn and her new bloke Freddie set off to Derbyshire.

"We're staying in the lodge." announced John proudly as they got out of the school mini bus. Nikki was thrilled. The lodge was usually reserved for corporate bookings when companies would send their employees on team building exercises or courses.

"Not only that," he added "we're being catered for too."

"By who?" asked Nikki

"Jo and a couple of the others offered."

"Really?" She was nothing if not a little surprised. "I didn't think Jo liked me very much."

"Whatever made you think that?" asked Suzanne.

"Some bitchy comments she made in the past."

"Well, she's offered so she couldn't have meant anything by it" As the friends walked from the car park to the lodge it became obvious to Nikki why Jo had offered.

"Happy birthday to you!" boomed Pip across the field. He broke into a jog, swinging a bottle of champagne in his hand. "Good trip everyone? Great to see you Nik. Happy belated birthday" and as he said this the champagne cork popped from the bottle and sprayed the contents all over her face.

"Do be careful." fussed Tom rather annoyed as he tried to mop her dry with his sleeve.

"Get off," laughed Nikki "It's fine. Lovely thought Pip, thank you." she said and took an enormous swig from the bottle. Pip beamed and did the same.

"Lighten up Tom, no harm done." joked Pip. They made their way to the lodge and unpacked. Nikki stood on the veranda. It was a beautiful evening, the sun was low in the sky and the smell of beef stew wafted across the quiet, unspoilt view of the distant hills. This was going to be a great weekend. And it was.

After Sunday lunch the group decided to go for a walk along the river track.

"I'm sorry" said Nikki regretfully "I think I'm going to have to sit this one out, my knee is giving me a bit of jip."

"Oh God Nik, you've over done it haven't you?" Suzanne looked worried.

"I'm okay Suze, really, I've learnt to know my limits, that's all. You lot go I'll finish the washing up and I've got a new book I haven't even started yet."

"I'm not leaving you on your own."

"I'm fine Suze, go."

"Ready then" piped up Tom. He had no intention of staying behind. He was a bit funny like that. He would fuss over Nikki and tell her what she could and couldn't do but never let anything stop him doing what he wanted to do. Her mother thought he was caring and always saw the best in him. Nikki, however, sometimes saw it as selfish. He could at least have offered to keep her company, even though she didn't want him too.

"Well you won't be on your own Nik, I don't fancy it. I could do with a nap, truth be told" said Pip and he slumped back into the shapeless sofa.

"It's okay, I'll stay too." said Jo. She just wanted to be wherever Pip was.

"For Christ sake, will you all just go," shouted Pip

for comic effect. "the wench has chores to do and this old bugger needs a kip."

Reluctantly Jo joined the others as they set off across the field.

"I'll put the kettle on."

"Lovely," smiled Pip as he settled back in the sofa "Do you want a hand?" The question was so half- hearted Nikki smiled. Pip looked tired and he had no intention of helping. After she'd finished clearing up, she took him cup of tea. Sitting down on the sofa next to him, Pip suddenly woke up.

"Sorry, didn't mean to disturb you. Here's your tea."

"Just resting my eyes." The two of them sat together talking about everything and anything. Despite their nineteen year age difference, it was surprising just how much the two of them had in common. They shared the same friends, he knew her family, her place of work, they liked the same type of music. In fact they didn't really have a difference of opinion on anything. Nikki felt like she had known him all her life. Up until now, they had never really been completely alone together, not for any length of time anyway. She felt so at ease with him, far more so than she had ever done, with anyone before.

"Things seem to be going well with Tom?"

She didn't really know why but Pips statement annoyed her.

"Yeah, I suppose so."

"Oh, you don't sound too keen." laughed Pip. "I thought you too were an item?"

"Well we *are*, we've been going out since Christmas. He's sweet and reliable and looks after me."

"That's good isn't it?"

"Yes. I just don't know if that's enough"

"Does he love you?"

"Yes."

"Do you love him?"

Nikki hesitated, "Yes. Yes in a way, I think I do. He just doesn't make me feel *that* feeling"

"What feeling's that then?"

"The feeling you get when you *really* love someone. When they are all you can think about, when they are the only one you want however silly or impossible that might be."

Pip took a sip of tea and put his cup down on the carved coffee table.

"Oh *that* feeling," he said, "and have you *ever* felt that feeling?" Pip looked straight into her eyes. Nikki looked straight back at him and held her gaze.

"You *know* I have."

Pip smiled and moved closer to her.

"I hoped you had" he said softly.

Nikki knew if she didn't say it now, she might never say it.

"Can I kiss you?" she whispered

"I thought you'd never ask." he said as he pulled her towards him. Their kiss was passionate and sincere but brief. Nikki pulled away and jumped up from the sofa.

"What's wrong?"

"This is. I should never have done that, I want you even more now. I know I can't have you, you're *married*, and I've just made the whole situation worse. This is a bloody mess and I'm really sorry."

"Stop it Nik, don't get upset." Pip stood up and went

over to her. He put his arms round her waist and snuggled his face in her neck.

"We both want it don't we? I think we've both known that for a long time. You can have me if you want too?"

"But not completely, can I Pip? I *love* you."

"I know" he said and kissed her lips. This time the kiss lasted. He wanted her as much as she wanted him. But there was no time, the others could be back at any moment and no one else could ever know what had just gone on between them.

The next morning they all packed up to leave.

"See you in the summer!" shouted Jo as they pulled away from the site. Pip had left early that morning as he had a big job on that week.

"Did you enjoy your birthday treat then sis?" asked Suzanne

"*Brilliant*! thank you, all of you - well worth waiting for."

"How's your knee this morning?"

"It's okay."

"Good job you didn't come on the walk yesterday afternoon" said Tom "It was quite strenuous, you would never have managed it." Nikki felt patronized. She knew he probably meant it kindly but he really did have the most annoying way about him sometimes.

"Yes, I'm *really* glad I didn't." she said, smiling to herself. She should have felt guilty about Pip, but she didn't. She had waited a long time for that kiss and so, it seemed, had he. One way or another she was going to have him. Just where, when and how and to what degree remained to be seen but she knew that this weekend had triggered the inevitable between them. They were meant to be together.

Chapter Thirteen

Preparations for the summer trip to the activity centre were being finalized, as they always were, in the pub. John, Suzanne, Tom, Pip, Mick and Rosie were sitting at their usual table. Nikki was working until eight and was to join them later. As it turned out, it was nearer ten when she eventually walked in.

"Where have you been?" Tom said with more than a little annoyance in his voice. Tom liked everything to be just so and expected everyone else to want the same. Time schedules were there for a reason.

"Sorry everyone," smiled Nikki as she plonked herself down next to Suzanne "We had some late arrivals at the hotel and I had to make them a bit of supper."

"That's not your job," snapped Tom "where were the kitchen staff?"

"They've all finished for the night, and anyway I don't mind."

"You are far too easily put upon, you need to stand up for yourself and stop letting people take advantage of you."

"We all help each other out, it's no big deal, I really didn't mind."

"Maybe you should start minding," continued Tom who seemed dead set on having an argument "Doesn't it matter to you that you have let your friends down this evening?"

Nikki looked stunned and Pip could see she was uncomfortable.

"Oh don't be so mellow dramatic, Tom." interrupted Pip "I'm in the chair Nik, what can I get you to drink?"

"I'll give you a hand." she said, as she got up to go to the bar with Pip.

"I'm sorry if I've let you all down" she said

"Of *course* you haven't. Tom's just fussing like he always does, he wants all the T's crossed and the I's dotted, you know what he's like. God knows how you put up with him sometimes."

"He's alright, really" Nikki replied trying to believe her own words. Pip smiled at her.

"I've got a proposition for you. You don't have to do it but I thought I'd ask you first"

"Go on I'm intrigued"

"I'm fitting a new kitchen in a mate's house, bit of a favour for him, he's doing up the place to let out. The down side is he wants it finished by the weekend."

"Where do I fit in?"

"You've got three days off this week, haven't you?"

"Yes, how did you know that?"

"It's how the hotel rotas work, if you're on 'til eight this week, you've got three shifts until midnight starting tomorrow and then three days off" he grinned at her "It's the sort of stimulating stuff Pat and I talk about. Well, she talks and I try and look interested. I know more about that bloody hotel than the owner. Anyway, now I have an interest, I've started to listen."

"So what do you want me to do?"

"Be the Chippy's mate," grinned Pip. "Hold up the cupboards while I fix them to the wall that sort of thing, you up for it?"

"Where's those drinks?" called John

"Coming right up" Pip called back "Think about it?" he said to Nikki and carried the tray of drinks over to the table. The meeting concluded shortly afterwards and Tom stood up to leave.

"Come on Nikki time to go, I've got an early start in the morning" he said getting his jacket. "She's only just got here," said Pip, "perhaps she'd like another drink?" Before Nikki had the chance to say anything, Tom had made his way to the door.

"If she likes." he said and left. Everyone turned to look at Nikki.

"Don't ask," she said "you all know what he's like at times. Bit of spoilt brat who sulks if he doesn't get his own way."

"White wine?" Pip made his way back to the bar. Soon only Suzanne, John, Pip & Nikki remained. After half an hour or so John stood up,

"We'd best be making a move," he said "You ready Nik?"

"Actually there's a couple of things I need to discuss with Nik ready for this week, I'll drop her off on my way home. You two go on. See you soon" said Pip.

"Oh yeah?" smiled John "What are you up to Philip?"

Pip laughed. "Nikki's going to give me a hand fitting

that kitchen in Rob's place this week, as she's got a bit of time off."

"Are you?" Suzanne looked amazed.

"Don't be so surprised," Nikki grinned at John "I was good at woodwork wasn't, I Mr Rowland?"

"First class. We'll leave you two, to it then. Goodnight."

Nikki looked round the pub. Apart from the landlord and one regular old chap who never moved from the stool at the end of the bar, she and Pip were the only ones left. Pip sat close to her. His smile made her heart pound. She really loved this man. She wanted to kiss him but it wouldn't be right, not in a public place. He knew what she was thinking.

"I'll pick you up at eight on Wednesday morning. You're bound to get dirty so wear some old stuff, that you won't mind getting messed up. Now, that's the business out the way. Let's get out of here." Pip led Nikki out toward his van.

"Where are we going?"

"Don't know, don't care, just somewhere I can have you all to myself for a while."

They drove through the town and were soon heading out into the countryside. After a couple of miles, Pip swerved into the dirt track entrance of a field. He switched off the engine and turned to Nikki.

"Come here." he said as he pulled her towards him and kissed her so passionately that she felt like a helpless rag doll.

"I want to make love to you, Nikki, I've wanted to since the first time you kissed me, but, if you don't want to I understand. As long as you realize I'm going to ask you every chance I get until you do."

"You know I do. I've thought about making love with you for as long as I can remember. You're my fantasy Pip."

"Wow, no pressure then!"

"None at all" she said as she settled back in the passenger's seat. He moved over towards her kissing her neck as she undid the belt on his trousers.

"It's okay" she said nervously "I'm on the pill."

Pip laughed. "Well every precaution taken there then, I've had the snip" Nikki stopped what she was doing for a minute. Nikki remembered that some time ago Danny had told her Pip couldn't have children but not for this reason.

"Have you?" she was a little surprised and disappointed. "Why?"

"After Carrie was born, Pat had a dreadful time, so decided I should get the snip."

"Oh that seems *fair*" Nikki replied sarcastically. "What a waste. Don't you wish you'd had kids of your own?"

"Have you been listening to gossip? he asked.

"Sorry. None of my business."

"We all have regrets sometimes Nikki, but dwelling on them doesn't change anything. At the time, having a vasectomy seemed like a good idea, it's too late now. Look, do we have to talk about this? It's not doing a lot for my libido."

Pip seemed a little sad and Nikki wished she hadn't said anything. She pulled him towards her again. They wrestled to change places as Pip managed to get himself into her seat, but not before he'd sounded the horn, twice, and banged his knee on the gear leaver. They were giggling like a couple of school kids. The moon light, shone across his face. He looked a lot younger than his thirty seven years.

"Pity." she whispered as she lowered herself onto him.

"What is?" he asked.

"I think I would have quite liked to have your children." she giggled. Nikki wanted him inside her. She had wanted it for such a long time, imagined how he would feel and how good it would be. He pushed himself up hard and deep inside her and they made love. Hard, fast and urgently. It was over far too quickly.

"I'm sorry Nik" he said as pushed her off him and climbed back into the driving seat.

"Please, don't be. I've wanted you for so long" she answered gently. Pip started the van.

"That was crap" he said. Nikki felt a little hurt.

"It wasn't, Pip."

He drove her back home fast and in silence. She began to think it was her fault.

"Did I do something wrong?" she asked as they pulled up outside the house.

"No, *I* did." He leant across her and opened the door. She went to kiss him goodnight but he moved away.

"Not here, someone might see us." His mood had really changed and Nikki felt awkward. She didn't want to get out of the van, but the engine was running and she thought it might disturb the neighbours.

"Do you still want me to help this week?"

"Yes of course. See you Wednesday, eight o'clock, be ready."

"I will." she said as she shut the van door and fumbled for her key. She went straight up to her bedroom and lay on her bed. Whatever it was she expected to feel after making love to the man of her dreams for the first time, should have felt an awful lot better than what she was feeling right now. Why did she feel so bad? She got undressed and ready for bed, snuggled up tight pulling the covers over her head and not for the first time, cried herself to sleep.

By the time she arrived at work the following morning, Nikki was much happier. After all, the night before she had made love with Pip. The man nineteen years her senior, the man she had always loved and the man she thought was out of her reach. It may not have been the greatest sex but it was by far the most momentous in her young life and the only time it had really meant anything to her.

"Good morning hen" Danny's usual cheery voice greeted her as she entered the lobby of the *Railway View* hotel. "You look happy, what have you been up too?"

Was it that obvious? She hoped not, what happened last night was to be kept secret from everyone. No one could know, especially in the work place. After all, Pip's wife worked here. Nikki was going to find this so very difficult to keep to herself. She would *have* to tell someone.

"I'll tell you later, if you're good" she smiled.

"Oooh, now I'm intrigued. Set your watch hen, you and me, three fifteen in the rest room. Be there!"

The day had passed slowly and Nikki was glad when eventually it was time for the afternoon tea break. She poured the tea as Danny came in and sat at the small table resting his feet on the chair opposite.

"Well here I am hen, spill. Something's put a smile on your face, tell me all about it"

"All about what?" said Pat as she rinsed her mug under the tap. Nikki glared at Danny.

"Nothing," said Nikki "You know what Danny's

like you've only got to smile and he thinks you're up to something" Danny looked confused.

"You said, I'll tell you later, I've been wondering all day, what was I 'sposed to think?"

"Have we got any custard creams left?" Nikki asked Pat trying to distract from a conversation she didn't want to have.

"No I scoffed the last four with my coffee" replied Pat as she left the room.

"Well thanks for sharing." Danny called after her as the door closed "Piggy!"

"You nearly dropped me right in it." whispered Nikki

"Now what have I done?"

"It's what *I've* done."

"Oh yeah, tell me more, I knew you were up to something."

"It's Pip"

"Pat's Pip?" asked Danny

"Yes, if you must. How many Pip's do we know?" Nikki replied sarcastically.

"What's Pip? What do you mean Nik? Oh God. You mean it's Pip! You haven't, have you? Oh yes she has! Bloody hell Nikki, are you insane? Pat will *kill* you, she *will* you know, she will *actually* kill you. She's got one hell of a temper. Tell me I'm wrong?" Danny looked genuinely distressed."It's a very dangerous game you're playing young lady."

"I *love* him Danny, I have done for years. I thought that it was just a fantasy and he was out of my reach, until last night."

"You can't *love* him Nikki. He's married to Pat. Alright, so it's plain for all to see that he might be tempted to look elsewhere but that doesn't alter the fact he is married. Plus he's far too old for you. And what about Tom? Remember him? Where does he fit into all this?"

"Okay! I get it, you don't approve, forget I told you." She got up and cleared away her cup.

"You knew how I felt about him. I really tried not to, you know that. I just wanted to share it with someone and you are my best friend. I can't tell anyone else."

"Look, hen, I just don't want to see you get hurt, you mean the world to me. Just be careful" Danny's look of horror turned to a wry grin. "I must admit though, I've always thought it a shame that those fine loins weren't being utilized!"

Nikki smiled. "I can't explain why I feel the way I do about him, I've just always felt a really strong connection to him and now it seems he feels it too. I can't walk away from that Danny, I can't, I won't, I don't want to."

"He is gorgeous hen, no denying that. But don't you *dare* tell another soul. Promise me?"

"I promise"

"Pat really would kill you, I mean it. She's unhinged" Danny believed what he was saying and it suddenly hit home to Nikki that this could well be true. It still wasn't enough to stop her. Not now.

Nikki joined her father for breakfast the following morning.

"To what do I owe this great honour?" said Derek sarcastically. It was a rare occurrence these days for them to share the first meal of the day, especially on her day off.

"I'm helping Pip today, we're fitting a kitchen." she said proudly. Derek laughed.

"He must be desperate! Why's he asked you?"

"He's got to have it finished by the weekend and I have a bit of spare time. Makes sense"

"Does he realize you'll be more of a hindrance than a help?"

"He doesn't seem to think so" Nikki retorted. The door bell rang and Marion brought Pip through to the kitchen.

"Good morning all" beamed Pip. "Have you got any idea what you're letting yourself in for?" joked Derek.

"John assures me her woodwork 'O' level was justly earned"

"Just don't let her near anything that needs precision. She can't keep to a line, never could, blames the tools because she's left- handed."

"I'm left handed too. I suffered the same problem so I use left handed tools as much as possible." he winked at Nikki. "Right handed people just don't seem to appreciate that we have to be far more skilled than them to survive in this discriminative world."

Nikki beamed. At last she had an ally.

"You're as daft as she is," laughed Derek. "you two make a great pair. Best of luck, you're going to need it."

"You ready then?"

"Ready." said Nikki

"Wait a minute," called Marion "I've made you both some sandwiches."

"Wow, thank you very much, Marion. That's a real first for me." Pip kissed her cheek and Marion blushed slightly.

"Doesn't your wife make you any?"

"No, no she never has. Bye then. Thanks again"

"I would" said Nikki as they got in the van.

"You would what?"

"Make you sandwiches. Everyday" smiled Nikki.

"Yes, I bet you would" he smiled.

Pip was a very skilled carpenter and by the time they stopped for their packed lunch, all the base units were fitted except for the doors.

"You've proved to be a great help, we'll be finished by tomorrow at this rate."

"Pity," replied Nikki "I was looking forward to spending three days with you."

"Well you still can, just two of them will have to be in the kitchen."

"So where will the other one be?"

"In every other room in the house, we should make the most of this." he grinned as he pushed her down on to the dusty floor covered in sawdust. Nikki started to laugh. He couldn't be serious. This was madness.

"Get your jeans off." he said and pulled a large dust sheet off the worktop for her to lay on. Nikki felt an immense rush of excitement. This was messy, this was risky and this was a huge turn on. Pip stood over her and dropped his jeans and boxers to the floor. He looked amazing. He was so big and Nikki wanted him so much. He lowered himself onto her gently and this time he took it slowly as he pushed himself inside her tight young body. He was wonderful. She soon felt herself ready to come and urged him to go harder and faster. It was the first time she had experienced an orgasm at the same time as her lover.

It was the first time for him too.

"God, Nik. Wow! That was fantastic!" he gasped as he rolled off of her and straight onto the handle of a screwdriver.

"Shit!" he yelped.

"What's the matter?"

"I think we need a bit of comfort" he said pulling the tool from underneath him.

"I don't care where we are as long as we can be together"

Pip kissed her and they lay together for a short while before he got up.

"Better get on, I want that frame work up this afternoon before we leave"

Nikki got dressed and made them both a cup of tea. She was *loving* this, just her and Pip, working together, being together, making love together. It was all she had ever wanted and for now at least, she had got it. They laughed and sang along to the radio all afternoon and the time passed far too quickly.

"That's us done for the day" he said as he screwed the last fitting into the wall.

"Well, almost" and he pulled her towards him. "I don't have to be home for another hour." He kissed her hard and the sawdust that covered them earlier, got in her hair all over again.

"Hi Mum" called Nikki as she went into the house.

"How did you get on?" came the reply "Is Pip with you?"

"No he had to be home by five but said to thank you again for the sandwiches"

"Same again tomorrow?"

"That'll be great mum, thanks."

"You'd have thought his wife would have made an effort" Marion went on.

"Not if you knew her." said Derek as he came into the kitchen. "She's an odd sort. Chalk and cheese them two. I've often wondered why he puts up with her. Having said that though he seems to be able to do what he likes. Look at all the time he puts into the charity things he does. What with the holiday camps and the shows I don't suppose they see a great deal of each other so, perhaps it suits them both"

Nikki hadn't really given it much thought before. It was true, Pip was hardly ever at home. The only reason he had to be home this evening was because Pat had agreed to cover a shift at short notice. That had annoyed him as she hadn't organised any child care before she'd agreed to it.

"So how did you get on?" asked Derek "Has Pip still got all his digits... and *marbles* come to that?"

"We're getting on fine thank you. I had a great day, learnt a lot as it goes. I really enjoyed it" "Perhaps you should take up a trade then my girl....."

"Perhaps I might. I could be a sparkie or a plumber. You, me and Pip could have a whole kitchen installation business sewn up?" laughed Nikki

"You know that isn't a bad idea." said Derek thoughtfully.

"It *is* Dad, believe me, it is. I would never last a day working with you! I'm off for a bath"

"You *need* one" said Marion "your hair is full of sawdust" Nikki smiled to herself as she went to run the bath. She lay and soaked for nearly an hour, quiet and alone with only the thought of the wonderful day she had just spent with Pip. Her dreams were broken with a call from her mother to say that Tom had arrived. She didn't rush. She didn't particularly want to see him. She reluctantly got out of the bath and made her way to her bedroom to get dried. It was another half hour before she went into the living room, wearing a baggy, well-worn tee shirt and tracksuit bottoms.

"Hi Nikki" he said looking at her clothing "You do know we're going out tonight?"

"No. Are we? Where are we supposed to be going?"

"I told Mick and Rosie we'd go bowling with them. Hurry up and get changed."

"I *hate* bowling. You know that, it puts a hell of a strain on my knees."

"Well I've told them we'll go now. You can watch if you can't do it. Don't let me down"

"Oooh that *will* be fun. I'm not going Tom. I've had a busy day. I just want my dinner and a quiet night in."

"I don't want to stay in. You're not the only one who had a busy day. I've had a long day at work and want to let off a bit of steam and have a couple of pints. Are you coming or not?"

"Not."

"Goodnight Mrs Edwards" said Tom as he left "Maybe I'll see you tomorrow Nicola"

"You could have made a little more effort" said Marion.

"Why? He *always* does this. He never consults me and then gets annoyed if I don't want to do exactly as he wants. He's like a spoilt kid sometimes."

"He thinks the world of you. Just try a little bit harder. A bit of give and take goes a long way in a relationship"

"I *know* Mum. It's just that most of the time he takes and the only thing he gives *me* is orders." The truth was she felt Tom was getting in the way right now. For these three days she had Pip and she neither wanted nor needed anyone else.

The kitchen was finished by the following evening. Pip parked outside Nikki's house and squeezed her hand as she went to get out of the van.

"I've got a job I need to do in the morning but I should be finished by two. I'll pick you up then and we can see to any finishing touches" he said with a grin. Although she felt disappointed at their time being cut short she would at least have the following afternoon with him. Any time was better than nothing.

Nikki longed for every moment she could spend with Pip.

Their relationship continued to grow over the next four years. They found various ways to be together. Sometimes on the odd job, but these were very few and far between. On one occasion they even met at his house. Nikki felt this extremely uncomfortable and was really scared they'd get caught. Pip seemed to think it just added to the excitement.

There was no doubt about the attraction between them but she knew Pip was too set in his ways to change the situation. She had learnt early on not to try and discuss any future they might have together. He would get annoyed and tell her not to spoil things. She had accepted that the small amount of time they actually spent together was something to be cherished and she would rather have him on his terms than not at all. So that was how it stayed. She would go weeks, sometimes months without hearing from him, let alone seeing him, but despite this her love for him remained strong and true.

Chapter Fourteen

Her relationship with Tom had also grown. She loved him too. Not in the way she loved Pip, but she defiantly cared about him and most of the time, they enjoyed being together. So when he suggested they got engaged Nikki didn't see any reason not to. Everyone else in their circle of friends, were paired off. It made sense for them to do the same. They brought their first home, a modest two bed roomed end terraced house close to his parents and his work. Tom was sensible, safe and wanted nothing more than to settle down and start a family. He adored Nikki and when she accepted his proposal of marriage he couldn't have been happier.

Pip showed none of these qualities. He took risks, he was exciting, funny and sexy and for all the good it did her, she loved him like she could never imagine loving anyone else. But a long term future with him just wasn't to be, however much she wanted it. Despite her feelings, she married Tom in the spring of eighty five and rightly or wrongly could see no reason that this should change anything between her and Pip.

Setting up home together was fun, challenging and exciting. For the most part, anyway. Tom's true self became more prominent. For his age he was a surprisingly old fashioned man, with old fashioned values. He *expected* Nikki to pack his lunches, everyday, have a meal ready each evening, despite the fact she continued to work full time at the hotel. It was also down to her to do all the house work & gardening, which most of the time, was fine, but sometimes felt a little unfair. Tom saw himself as the provider. He was obviously far better paid than she was and often made her feel like her work was completely meaningless. Between them they decorated and renovated. Nikki was good at this and it was feeling she had achieved something in the home that kept her going in the early days. Tom would often be sent off to work at other branches of the bank, away from home. He also took time off from work to continue helping with the charity camps, as he always had and saw no reason to change. Nikki didn't have the same holiday allowance and consequently meant she was often left home alone. She missed the camps and the fun they used to have but her life had changed and some things had to give. She took these opportunities to catch up with friends, play the music she liked at the volume she wanted, took long baths, without being reminded of wasting water and generally did all the things Tom didn't like her doing. She preferred him working away, rather than the charity trips. She would have liked to be included in the trips but this never seemed to pan out. It also made her jealous that Tom was away with Pip. Well, it made her *annoyed*, more than jealous. As far as she was concerned it was a wasted opportunity for her and Pip to be together. But this was more than made up for when Tom was working away.

Tom was in Newcastle. He had been there for three out of the five day trip on the day Nikki had been sent home from work. She generally felt unwell but didn't know why and was having pain and spasms in her abdomen. She got home and made a cup of tea and curled up on the sofa. The pains got worse and before long to her horror and dismay, she realized she was having a miscarriage. Alone, frightened and heartbroken, she telephoned her mother.

Marion and Derek were there within minutes and called the doctor. There was nothing much anyone could do. Nikki lost the eleven week baby she hadn't realized she was carrying.

The doctor advised her to rest and assured her that she should begin to feel better in a day or so and that she should visit the surgery the following week.

Nikki wanted Tom. So she called the bank in Newcastle. She needed him to be at home with her. A woman answered the phone who abruptly told her, that Mr Denton wasn't to be disturbed. So Nikki left a message to say he needed to contact home urgently.

It was another hour and a half before he called her back.

"What's up, Nikki? I've got a message to call you."

"I want you to come home Tom, I've lost our baby," Nikki couldn't hold back the tears.

"What? You didn't say you were pregnant...."

"Please come home Tom, I need you."

"Why didn't you tell me?"

"I didn't know, well not for sure."

"You must have done."

"No, it's all a bit of a shock, please come home." There was a bit of a pause, while the news sunk in.

"Is your Mum there with you?"

"Yes, they've been here all afternoon. They said they'd wait until you got back."

"I can't just come back Nik, I've got stuff that needs doing here. You'll be alright won't you? You've got your Mum. You'll feel a lot better in a couple of days. I'll be back Friday night."

"But I want you with me Tom. *Please, please* come home."

"Put Marion on, I need to speak to her." he said.

Nikki handed the phone to her mother before curling up hugging a cushion close to her chest. She pushed her face into the cushion and sobbed.

A few moments later, Marion put the receiver down.

"He'll be back on Friday night, sweetheart. There's nothing he can do here. He needs to finish the job in Newcastle. I'll stay with you this evening."

Nikki couldn't believe Marion was defending him. Was it unreasonable to want your husband by your side in this situation? Nikki felt un-loved and very lonely. Marion put her to bed around eight o'clock and promised to call her in the morning.

"But if you need me during the night, you just ring." she said as she left her daughter to sleep. Nikki cried herself to sleep and despite everything slept soundly until around eight thirty the following morning. Still feeling exhausted she started to make her way to the shower, when the phone rang. She expected it to be Marion. It wasn't.

"Hi gorgeous," said Pip, "you busy this morning? I thought I could pop round for breakfast, as you're on a late shift today. Don't bother getting dressed!"

Nikki burst into tears.

"Whatever's the matter?" asked Pip deeply concerned. Nikki had barely said the word 'miscarriage' when Pip said he was on his way.

Pip shut the door behind him, hugged Nikki tight and let her cry into his chest until she could let go.

"I'll put the kettle on," he said "you sit yourself down." He brought the coffee through to the living room and sat close to her on the sofa. He was gentle and kind and he made Nikki feel safe. He was also absolutely furious that Tom hadn't been there for her. They talked and she cried, alot. He understood that this is just what she needed to do. Pip sat quietly stroking Nikki's hair, she felt like a little girl, quite unable to cope with everything.

"Is your Mum coming over today?" he asked after about an hour, and just as he did, Marion rang. Nikki couldn't let on Pip was there. She told her she was just getting up and about to have a shower and she would be okay on her own until Marion brought some lunch round about noon. Pip stayed until eleven. He felt awful leaving her alone and promised to ring later that afternoon. He gently kissed her as he left and told her if she ever needed him, he would be there for her, as much as he could, at least. The fury that Nikki felt for Tom had diminished somewhat. Not because she was starting to forgive him, that *really* was going to take some time, but because of the love and comfort Pip had shown her. She wouldn't have got through this without him and she loved him all the more for it. It was the first time, for a long while, that they had been together without making love and somehow that seemed to prove that their relationship was so much more than just sex.

By the time Tom got home Friday evening, Nikki didn't want to talk to him. Marion tried to act as a peace maker and eventually left them to it to sort their differences out. Derek had told her not to interfere, but Nikki could really have done with her support. Tom really didn't see why she had needed him at home, if she had her mum there. He also didn't seem to understand her up set of losing a baby they didn't know they were having.

"If you're really that upset we can try for another one." he said after a long silence at dinner the next day. Nikki left the table. He really had no idea how she felt and she didn't have the energy to argue.

Monday morning Nikki went back to work. She was covering reception most of the week and had confided in both Danny and Mrs Pyke about what had happened. They both felt sad for her and were very supportive. Tom, on the other hand, just didn't think there was anything to talk about. It was just one of those things and that was that.

As the weeks went by things went back to normal. Although Nikki began to feel better she now realized that what she really wanted most from life, was her own family. It wasn't long before she fell pregnant again. This time, she knew within a few of weeks. Tom was delighted but didn't want anyone else to know until she had gone past twelve weeks. So they kept it to themselves. Well, almost. Nikki had to tell Pip. She felt she owed it to him. Pip was really pleased for her and said she'd make a wonderful mum. Part of her wanted Pip to be jealous but he wasn't. He wanted her to be happy in her marriage with her own family. Something she could never have with him. The truth was, if he had asked, Nikki would have sacrificed everything for him. Pip knew that, and in time, Nikki realized it was because he loved her, that he never asked.

Charles Thomas Denton (Charley) made his debut in the world safely, on time and with very little fuss. Nikki found herself totally overwhelmed with love for this beautiful new life, and by the time she brought her son home from the maternity unit, she realized her life needed to change. Obviously, things were never going to be the same again. For one thing, Tom had insisted she was to be a stay –at-home mum and they were lucky enough to be in a position to allow her to do that. Tom had always planned to support his family. Nikki's earnings had always brought the extra things for the home and wasn't needed for the mortgage. Yes, they would have to cut down on a few luxury items and a new baby was expensive, but they would manage. That had all been discussed and planned. What Nikki hadn't planned on was how this little boy could alter all she felt for everything and everyone in her life. She decided very quickly that after their five year affair, her relationship with Pip had to end. All she needed to do was avoid him. That wasn't really that difficult. Sometimes they would go weeks without seeing each other. She would just make sure she wasn't going to be anywhere he was likely to be.

Simple.

Leaving the Railway View Hotel wasn't hard either. She had really enjoyed her time there. Work had often been hard and tiring, with long hours, but Danny had always made it fun and they would always stay friends. But she had a new role now. A new job. The best job. A constant twenty four hours a day, seven days a week, brilliant job. This suited both her and Tom. He had what he always wanted, a wife and son to come home to. Someone to look after him, to cook and clean for him and make sure his shirt sleeves had a crisp crease every day. Someone, who would be there to keep house while he continued to do what he always did. The truth was, his life hadn't changed much at all. It was just better for him, he was in control and he had Nikki where he wanted her. At home. Work continued to take him away every now and again and the charity camps and shows took up just as much time as they always had done.

Charley was two months old when Tom told Nikki they were having a planning meeting for the summer camp at the house the following evening.

"You can put on a bit of a spread and we can make an evening of it" Tom told her.

Everyone due to be there, had already met Charley, their friends had all been generous and supportive as Charley was the first of the next generation to arrive. They all doted on him. The only person who hadn't seen him was Pip.

Pip was going to come to the house. That was fine, she could handle it. It would make no difference. She was a mum now, and Pip had no place in her life. Well, yes he *did*, he was a friend. He just didn't have such a special place in her heart now.

"You need to go and get changed and smarten yourself up," instructed Tom "everyone will be here soon." Nikki was tired. She had been up all night as Charley had colic.

Despite having had very little time to herself all day, she had prepared a chilli for everyone to enjoy. She took Charley up to his Moses basket and left him beside her bed as she went into the bathroom to try and make herself look less exhausted than she actually was. Before she had closed the door, she heard Mick and Rosie arrive. Tom had shown them into the lounge and called up to her not to be too long. The warm water from the shower was relaxing and wonderful. Nikki was feeding Charley herself and had more than her fair share of milk. She spent most of the time with either rock solid breasts or very soggy clothing There didn't seem to be any in-between. The warm shower helped to relieve some of the pressure. As she was getting dry, Charley started to cry. This triggered another flow of milk and Nikki smiled to herself. What was the point in trying to get dry and tidy? Charley came first.

"Mummy's coming." she said as she left the bathroom in just her towel. But Charley had stopped crying. He was looking at the kind face of the man that had picked him up for a cuddle.

"Hello, mummy. We're just introducing ourselves. He's beautiful, Nik." smiled Pip. He looked tanned, handsome and incredibly gentle as he sat cradling Charley in the dimly lit room.

"What are you doing up here?" Nikki said rather annoyed as she took her son from him.

"Tom said I could come up when he heard the little fella crying as I arrived. He said you'd see to him after your shower, so I offered. I didn't think you'd mind?"

"Well I'm here now, you can go downstairs, thank you."

"What's up, Nik? Is that *it* then? Not even a hug?" Pip looked hurt.

"*Please* Pip, we can't do this anymore. It's not fair to *any* of us." Pip stood up from the side of the bed. He walked towards Nikki and the little bundle in her arms.

"You look wonderful sweetheart, motherhood suits you." He lent forward and kissed her forehead. The touch of his lips and the smell of his skin made Nikki go weak. She let him kiss her and snuggled her head into his chest.

"God, I want you." he said.

"Really, even like this? Nikki looked at herself. She was carrying extra weight; her breasts were huge and uncomfortable. She felt fat and frumpy and nothing seemed to be in the right place anymore. Her hair hung wet and scraggily and the dark rings under her eyes gave more than a hint of her tiredness. Pip sniggered.

"Especially like this, you really have no idea just how much of a turn on this is, I've really missed you, Nik." he said as he tried to pull open her towel. It was the first time in months she had felt desired. Tom had kept his distance since she had become pregnant. He said he was worried he would harm the baby. The truth was, he wasn't really interested in that side of their relationship. It didn't bother him. It hadn't bothered Nikki much either. She had always had Pip for the passion in her life. He was all she had ever wanted. But now that had to change. She grabbed her towel tight and moved back from him.

"I need to be here for Charley. I can't let anything spoil that, *please* Pip, don't make this any harder than it already is."

"If that's what you *really* want, I'll stay away, but only if you can look me in the eyes and tell me you don't love me."

Nikki looked up at him. "I can't do that, you *know* I can't."

Pip kissed her passionately on the lips.

"I wish he could have been mine." he whispered, as the tears rolled down her cheeks.

"Come on Nikki," Tom called up the stairs, "we're all waiting for you down here."

"Take your time Nik, I'll tell them you're feeding Charley." Pip smiled at her and bent to kiss her beautiful son.

"I hope you appreciate how lucky you are little man, I'd love to be in your babygro for the next few minutes." Pip winked at Nikki.

"Don't listen to the rude man," laughed Nikki, "He'll lead you astray." Nikki towel dried her hair and got herself comfortable on the bed to feed Charley. She could hear everyone downstairs and didn't really want to rush to join them. She looked lovingly at Charley as he contently fed from her. His soft perfect skin nestled up against her breast. She yawned with contentment. Se cherished these moments with just her and her son. The door bell made her jump and she heard her sister arrive. After a while, Suzanne went upstairs to see if Nikki was alright. She tip-toed into the bedroom and gently lifted her little nephew off of Nikki and laid him in the basket. Both Nikki and Charley were sound asleep. Suzanne pulled the blanket over her sister before creeping back down stairs.. She went in to the others.

"Bless her," she said" She's worn out."

"Where is she?" said Tom

"I left her asleep on the bed."

"How *bloody* rude." snapped Tom and he got up to go upstairs. Everyone went quiet and looked at each other.

"*Leave* her Tom, she needs to sleep." said Suzanne.

"She can do that tomorrow she doesn't have much else to do all day. We've got guests now and she has a meal to dish up."

"Whoa, steady *on* Tom, bit Victorian aren't you? The poor girls exhausted, anyone can see that. If it helps, I'll dish up." smiled Pip.

Tom looked annoyed. "Charles is nearly nine weeks, she should be okay by now" said Tom.

Pip laughed. "Ooooh, you *poor*, deluded sod."

Nikki slept until eleven thirty when Charley woke for another feed. Tom was just getting into bed.

"You embarrassed us tonight," he grunted. "You could have made more of an effort with our friends." Nikki didn't answer. She cuddled Charley and thought of Pip.

"I wish he could have been yours, too." she said silently to herself as the cold back of her husband pushed against her hip.

Chapter Fifteen

Over the next few years, the little Denton family grew. By the age of four, Charley had become a big brother to Harry. Tom continued to work for the bank and had got a promotion. Consequently his involvement with the charity had suffered and he saw their friends less and less. He worked long hours and often away from home.

Nikki loved being a mum. She devoted her time to the children and her home. Suzanne was a wonderful auntie and Marion and Derek were totally smitten with their grandchildren. Nikki didn't see much of their old friends. Her life had changed. She was the only one with children and as anyone will tell you, those *without*, lead very different lives.

For a while Pip had also been pushed into the background. Although he was never far from her thoughts, the risk of spoiling what she had was too great. She had told herself that the boys were all that she needed. She was a mum; she had a worth and a purpose. Something she had never felt as a wife. Pip would ring her occasionally and the two of them would talk about anything and everything and flirt outrageously, but Nikki declined the offers to meet up. If she didn't actually *see* him, she could control her feelings. And that seemed to work, for a *time* anyway.

Suzanne was to turn thirty in a few weeks time. She was planning a party at the *Locomotive*. This was a great opportunity to get everyone back together and catch up with old friends.

The evening arrived and Nikki was strangely apprehensive. Tom put it down to her *letting herself go* as he put it. True, she was a couple of stone heavier than before she had the children but was still fit and active nevertheless. Marion and Derek came to babysit. The idea of spending the evening at a disco, was not their idea of a good time, so they were glad to look after the boys instead. Besides which they had planned a special family dinner the following day for Suzanne at their home. Tom answered the door but hardly even acknowledged them. Nikki felt she had to apologize for his rudeness but Derek and Marion defended him, as they always did, saying he was a busy man with a lot on his mind. Nikki never did understand why they stuck up for him. They would have soon told *her* off if she behaved the way he did. Maybe they could already see the cracks in their relationship and were gently trying to smooth them over. Tom led the way into the pub function room. Nikki followed and was so relieved to be greeted by Danny. The hug was sincere and warm and Nikki instantly relaxed. Danny held on to her for a while and when he released his hold Nikki could see he was crying.

"Silly'ol bugger. Sorry, hen, promised myself I wouldn't,

not tonight. How are you? I don't think a day has passed since I've missed having you around."

"Oh Danny" she replied as she pulled him back for another hug, "Whatever is the matter?"

"I've lost my Bernie; the old fool went and died on me, I mean, how selfish eh?"

"I'm so sorry, Danny, I didn't know. When did it happen? Why didn't you *call* me? Nikki felt dreadful for not being there for her friend.

"About three months ago now hen. The big 'C', He had been under the hospital for while but never said a word. I miss him so much."

Nikki held him tight until he pulled away.

"So who's running this place now? She looked over to the bar where a couple in their forties were serving.

"Oooh, you ain't gonna believe this - wait for it - that's Bernie's *son* and daughter-in-law."

"Really?" exclaimed Nikki, "I thought he was....."

"Well, I know he was, darling!" grinned Danny "But hey ho, who knows what we get up to on our journeys through life. He never told me. Can't pretend it wasn't a bit of a surprise. Anyway, promise me we'll have coffee and a catch up in the week hen, tonight's about your Suzanne, so I'll go get us some drinks and let's have a boogie!"

Nikki watched Danny walk over to the bar. There was a time when he would have skipped but now she feared that time had passed. Danny was missing something that had given him extra sparkle and she hadn't been there for him. She doubted that anyone else had either.

"Well, long time no see. I'd hoped you'd be here." his

words sent tingles all through her body and as she turned round to look at Pip she felt like she might actually pass out.

"Of course I'm going to be here, I'd hardly miss my own sisters' party." she replied in an almost annoyed tone. Pip looked a bit confused.

"Are you alright, sweetheart?"

"Yes. No, sorry, that was rude of me. I've just had a bit of bad news and then you startled me, sorry."

"What's up?" Pip asked as he led her to a small table for two. She told him about Bernie and her guilt for not being there for Danny. Pip took her hand.

"We can't all be everywhere all the time, don't blame yourself. Danny won't."

She knew he was right. He was *always* right and knew just what to say. Tom came over to the table with a glass of orange juice and lemonade. He looked at Pip's hand holding Nikki's and said nothing. Pip didn't move.

"I saw Danny at the bar. He was getting you a very large white wine, but I told him you're not drinking anymore."

He put the drink on the table. Nikki stood up, said nothing, and went over to Danny.

"I think Tom picked up the wrong drink." she said and took the wine from Danny.

"That's my girl." he smiled.

She raised her glass high and made a toast to Bernie.

"To Bernie" echoed Danny, "Where ever you are, you ol' bugger!"

"What's up with her?" Tom asked Pip in a way that didn't really warrant a reply.

"Sometimes, Tom," said Pip as he rose to his feet, "you can be a such a shit."

He walked over to join Nikki and Danny at the bar. Pip knew how to lighten the moment. He took Danny's face in his hands and planted him a kiss, smack on the lips! Danny looked stunned and all three of them roared with laughter.

"Whey hey, things are looking up!" squealed Danny.

"My round." said Pip and Nikki accepted a second large glass of wine. She was with friends, true friends, *best* friends and, oh, *how* she'd missed them.

Chapter Sixteen

The following week, Nikki kept her word and met up with Danny. They had a long lunch together and chatted about the good ol' days at the *Railway View,* and the mischief the two of them got up to and Nikki felt like a naughty little girl again. It was great to see her friend laugh but something had changed in him and there was nothing she could do to alter that. They talked about Bernie and that was just what Danny needed to do.

"Anyway, that's enough about me, hen. So I presume from the other evening that it's still on with the gorgeous Philip?" Nikki looked a little shaken. Was it that obvious?

"We talk a lot Danny, but that's it. I can't risk messing up the family. I love Pip, you know I do, I always have and I think I always will. But I love my boys *more*. We can't be together anymore."

"Well, you keep telling yourself that love and one day you might actually believe it."

"I *do* mean it Danny, We can't see each other anymore." and as the words left her lips she couldn't stop the tears from rolling down her cheeks.

"Come here, hen" said Danny as he pulled her towards him and hugged her tight,

"Now you listen to me. If you are lucky in life, you find someone you truly love. The magic happens when you realize, that, that someone, loves you too. It's *rare*, Nik, and so, so special. Take it from an ol' fool who knows. Whatever people think, however hard it is, if you've found that *something* with someone, you bloody well fight for it."

"You've changed your tune." sniffed Nikki.

"I was trying to protect you before, but when I saw you two together last Saturday it is so obvious you two should be together."

"Maybe." smiled Nikki. She wanted to hang on to the thought that one day that just might come true, but deep down she didn't really believe it. Pip was her fantasy, he always *had* been. Admittedly she had been lucky to have had opportunities to live out that fantasy and that had only led to *enhancing* it. That was going to have to be enough. It had to be.

Tom was on a trip to Europe. The bank was planning on opening branches in both France and Portugal and, as project manager, he had travelled to France to see firsthand how the plans were progressing. He relished the responsibility and had been so focussed on this over the last few months he had hardly been at home. So when he packed to go away for eight weeks, neither, Nikki or the boys really missed him. Family life went on much the same, but Nikki invited Danny over every weekend for a meal and was so much happier to have her friend back in her life. She had Pip back too. He had called her after Suzanne's party and her efforts to keep apart from him were futile. She had also thought long and hard about her conversation with Danny. He was right. Love is worth fighting for. Why should they be miserable apart when they knew how happy they were together? Since Tom was away, it was easy to pick up where they had left off. She didn't even feel guilty, why should she? Tom didn't want her. She wasn't sure if he even loved her anymore. He never said he did. He certainly didn't *show* her he did. She felt like a house keeper for him, nothing more. Pip made her feel good about herself. She felt loved, she felt sexy, she felt like she wanted to feel and she had really missed that.

"I'm sorry Nikki but I can't see you for a couple of weeks." Pip said as he was getting dressed. They had just spent the evening in bed together, drinking wine and making love. The boy's were sound asleep in the next room and Nikki was content.

"We're going on holiday. She's booked a fortnight in Corfu, sorry"

"It's ok, Pip." she replied although she couldn't help but feel a little hurt. It didn't get any easier, after all these years she still didn't want to think of Pip having a wife.

"I'll be back before you know it."

"You'll be back after Tom, we won't get another chance like this for a while."

"I've been thinking about that. When did you last have a holiday?"

Nikki forced a smile. "Before the boys came along, I dunno. About six years ago, I guess?"

"*Really?*" exclaimed Pip. He loved his holidays, and wouldn't miss his annual weeks in the sun. He and Pat went abroad at least twice every year. Their daughter Carrie had left home two years ago at the age of fifteen, and despite the social services intervention, hadn't returned home. She had dossed down with various *friends* and once she had turned sixteen, the authorities pretty much washed their hands of her. No one seemed to know where she was for sure. Pat didn't seem that concerned and was making up for what she considered to be lost time. Without Carrie around to worry about, she now wanted to travel and was out more and more. She went away with a friend quite regularly and Pip continued to work to pay for her new found freedom. He was also sending money to Carrie, but had promised her he wouldn't let on to her mother.

"I'm not that bothered, really," Nikki continued "Mum and Dad are planning a trip to North Yorkshire this autumn, I think me and the boys will probably go with them."

"And Tom?"

"No."

"Do you ever do *anything* together?"

"No, it doesn't matter anymore. It used to annoy me, I wanted to be the *normal* family, whatever that is, but he just hasn't the time for us all. Don't get me wrong, he really loves our boys and I dearly wish he would spend more time with them, but his work seems to be his priority. It's a real shame, he misses so much" Nikki put on her dressing gown and led Pip down the stairs. They stood in the hallway. Pip took Nikki's face in his hands.

"How long have we been together, Nik?"

"Twelve years." she smiled.

"It's about time we spent a whole night together, don't you think?" Nikki was amazed. He had always made excuses as to why he couldn't and she had never pushed him. But she'd love that. To wake up next to him was all she had ever wanted to do.

"You make the arrangements while I'm away, go for a week day night, it's easier for me to get away then. Pick a good hotel, London, that should be easy enough." Pip beamed. "My treat"

With this to look forward to it made the fact he was away much easier to cope with. Tom was due home on the Monday and she planned her night away for the following Tuesday. She hated lying to Tom. She hadn't really had to lie before, just had to keep quiet and that wasn't the same as actually lying. She told him she was going to meet up with Lyn, her old school friend whom she hadn't seen for years. They were going to hit the shops and try and get some *returns* for one of Andrew Lloyd Webbers shows. Tom didn't see why they couldn't get the late train home, but Nikki pointed out that, as Lyn now lived in Brighton, she would have to travel back alone very late at night and she didn't want to do that. Marion had invited Tom and the boys over for tea and would pick up the boys in the morning. All Tom had to do was put them to bed and get them up, dressed, fed and ready for school. In fairness, he seemed genuinely pleased to have them to himself for a bit. He dropped Nikki at the station as she struggled hard not to show her excitement. The only pang of guilt she felt was when the high pitched giggly voices of Charley and Harry squealed out "Bye bye mummy, have a lovely time, we love you!"

"I'll ring you in the morning, before you go to school, be good for Daddy and grandma, I love you too."

"Have a nice time" said Tom as he drove away. The

slight feeling of guilt was quickly replaced with excitement as she boarded the 15.10 to Kings Cross. She felt like a child. Excited, nervous, and happy. She flipped the lid of her walkman open and inserted the CD Pip had told her to get. He had an LP of Dr. Hook called *'Pleasure and Pain'* and so many of their lyrics made him think of her. With the head phones firmly in place she listed to *Sharing The Night Together* and *I Don't Wanna Be Alone Tonight* with a smile that could have betrayed her secret. She couldn't wait to see Pip. As she watched the countryside speed pass the window, she suddenly had an overwhelming worry that he might not be there. What if he wasn't? What if he couldn't get away after all? What was she doing? He had insisted they travelled on different trains at different times, as they couldn't risk being seen together. But now she had no way of knowing if he would actually be there. Oh, well if he wasn't she'd just have to come straight back home. She got the tube to Green Park and made her way to the hotel on Mayfair. She confidently approached the reception desk and asked if Mr Scarrow had checked in.

"Not as yet madam, would you be Mrs Scarrow?"

"Yes" replied Nikki enjoying her new role, "May I have our key?"

"Certainly madam" the concierge flicked his fingers towards the bell boy and instructed him to take Mrs Scarrow's hand luggage to her room.

"Enjoy your stay with us. If you need anything at all, please don't hesitate to ask."

"Thank you' she smiled as she got into the lift. The room was spectacular. It made even the very best room at the *Railway View* look shabby in comparison. There were two king sized beds covered in crisp white lining with thick quilted pillows and covers. Two high backed arm chairs sat either side of a small table displaying fresh yellow roses. An ice bucket pedestal stood chilling a bottle of champagne and two crystal cut glasses glistened in the late afternoon sun that shone through the large French window. Nikki opened the door to the well stocked mini bar and the little fridge. Inside lay a small tray of six fine chocolates. The little white card with gold writing read *with compliments* and advertised the chocolatier in the Burlington Arcade. Nikki opened the door to the bathroom. It gleamed with white marble and gold leaf. The bath was shaped for two people to share comfortably and the heated rail boasted two thick white fluffy towels. This was *pure* luxury, the likes of which she had never experienced. She went back into the room and unpacked her things. Pip had said he may not get there until six. It was only just gone five o'clock so Nikki decided to take a bath before he arrived. She poured the complimentary creamy bath milk into the hot water and opened an individual white wine bottle from the mini bar, saving the champagne for his arrival. She lowered herself into the bubbles and lay there feeling like a princess, this was heaven. After about ten minutes or so, she heard the key in the door.

"Hellooooo. Nikki?"

"In here." she replied.

"Bloody hell Nik, this is some place isn't it?"

Nikki smiled,

"Hello you, good day at work dear?"

Pip laughed, "I'd love to come home to this every day."

He bent down and kissed her hard on the lips. She put bubbles in his hair and pretended to pull him in with her.

"Move over," he ordered as he threw his clothes to the floor and climbed in the bath with her.

"Turn round, I'll do your back." he said gently. Nikki turned round and wiggled her bottom up between his legs, He lathered the sponge and massaged the foam into her soft skin. No one had ever done that, she'd never had a bath with anyone before. But now it seemed the most natural thing in the world and wondered why she hadn't. She was so relaxed. Pip started to kiss her neck and then lifted her onto his lap, as he slid up hard inside her. It was gentle and sensual and not long before she came on him.

"You ok, darling" he said. Nikki could hardly speak. She turned and kissed him.

"I love you." she whispered and for the very first time he replied,

"I love you too, Nik."

She had never felt happier and more loved than she did right at that moment.

They put on the matching bath robes as Pip opened the champagne.

"I could get used to this." he smiled as he handed her the flute.

"Me too......I've got a surprise for you," said Nikki "Shut your eyes." She placed two tickets for the *Phantom Of The Opera* in his hand.

"Happy Christmas!" she whispered as she kissed his cheek.

"It's October, Nik."

"I know. But I can't buy you anything *decent* then can I? They're for tonight. We haven't got much time."

"It's a nice thought, Nik. But we'd really be cutting it fine now."

Nikki felt hurt.

"You always said it was one of the shows you wanted to see, I thought you'd be *pleased*."

"I'd rather stay here with you and make the most of the room. Anyway, we haven't eaten yet I need to keep my strength up." Pip laughed loudly and pulled Nikki down on the bed on top of him.

"I 'spose you're right. They cost a fortune Pip, bit of a waste of money."

"If you paid on you card you might be able to get them sold as returns." Pip took charge. He helped himself to Nikki's purse and found the card, rang the theatre and gave a feeble excuse about his wife being rushed into hospital. Within the hour the theatre returned the call saying they were pleased to be able to refund the money to Nikki's card, as the tickets had been snapped up.

"See no harm done." Pip smiled. "And anyway, it's not the same since Michael Crawford left the role."

Nikki felt foolish. She didn't know what to say. So he *had* seen it already. There were lots of things he had done which she didn't know about, why should he - she was only the other woman. He didn't tell her much about his and Pat's life together. She had assumed they didn't do nice things like theatre trips, that's the sort of thing you did with someone special.

But now she guessed she was wrong. They got dressed as

they drank the rest of the champagne and then made their way down to the restaurant.

"What's up, Nik" Pip took her hand over the dining table.

"I just wanted to be able to give you something nice, that's all." she said.

"Nikki, darling, us *being* here together tonight is the best present I could have. Please, that's all I want. We'd be taking a chance going out to the theatre. We could be seen together. It's not worth the risk. Let's not spoil this special night? We've waited too long for it,"

A few minutes after they had finished their main course, the waiter came over to them. He was tall with olive skin, deep brown eyes and jet black hair. He nodded to Pip and smiled at Nikki,

"Can I get you anything for dessert?"

His voice was smooth and deep and Nikki was quite mesmerised by him.

"I don't think you can," she said, "That was delicious but I'm really full." The truth was she knew what lay ahead for her that night and the last thing she wanted was a heavy stomach or indigestion.

"But madam," protested the waiter, "you will hurt the feelings of our pastry chef, he has created an assortment of wonderful desserts for beautiful ladies, just like you."

Pip smirked "He says that to *all* the girls."

"On the contrary Sir, I say that to very few. Your wife *is* beautiful and she should have only the very best."

Nikki blushed. She loved the fact the waiter thought she was Pips wife. She took Pip's hand,

"Are you going to have something, darling?" she asked

him. Pip couldn't choose. The waiter stood patiently and eventually Nikki said.

"Just the lemon parfait for me, please,"

Pip didn't really recognise anything else so said "same" and handed back the menu.

The waiter returned after ten minutes with a large silver oval tray. It was arranged with delicately placed miniature desserts from the entire range. Fourteen in all. All bite size and all exact replicas of the full size desserts.

"For you madam. With compliments of the chef. Enjoy." he smiled and looked intently at Nikki. "Brilliant!" laughed Pip, "I'm bringing you again. Do you know how much that would have cost? He likes you." and with that ate the lemon parfait in one mouthful.

The dinner had been perfect. Just being able to sit alone together, enjoying a meal, meant the world to Nikki. But the desire to have Pip again, was intense and before too long, they made their way up to the room. It was a little after nine when they got into bed, and for the next six hours, they made love.

Just before seven am, there was a knock at the door.

"You go." mumbled Pip. Nikki pulled on the bath robe and opened the door. A small man with an enormous tray stood there.

"Good morning, madam. Your breakfast." he stated as he entered the room. He put the tray on the table by the French windows and stood politely waiting for a gratuity. Pip lay in bed with the sheet barely covering his erection.

"Tip the man, Nik and come back to bed."

Nikki felt the blood rush to her cheeks, she hastily

gapped her purse and gave the man two pounds. As the door clicked shut, Nikki turned to Pip.

"Why did you say that? You made me feel like a tart?"

"You *are* my tart!" roared Pip. Nikki didn't laugh. "Oh come on, Nik, only joking."

Nikki turned away from him and poured the tea from the bone china tea pot.

"Tea or coffee?" she asked Pip

"Neither," he whispered into her neck and she felt her robe dropped to the floor

"That can wait, this can't....."

This time the sex was rough, fast and urgent. Nikki felt powerless and exhausted. He was fantastic. And she loved him.

As they finished breakfast, Pip said he was getting the 8.55 from Kings Cross.

"You don't have to rush back. We had better stick to separate trains anyway. You never know who we might bump into. I don't want anything to spoil this now."

Nikki knew not to push her luck, she had just spent the best night of her life with the man she loved and although that was now over, it would have to be enough for now.

She showered, got dressed and made her way down to the foyer of the hotel. She handed the key back to the concierge.

"I trust you enjoyed your stay Mrs Scarrow?" he smiled as he took the key from her.

"Yes thank you, very much." she replied,

"Congratulations on your anniversary. A pity Mr Sparrow has been called back for work."

This was typical of Pip, he'd obviously spun him some

sort of line before he left. Nikki smiled. "Happens all too often." she replied happy to back up her *husband's* story.

"So, just the matter of your bill, madam."

Nikki looked stunned. Pip had said his treat, hadn't he? He must have forgotten. Sod him, she only had her credit card and although she could easily explain theatre tickets, how was she going to justify a two- hundred- and –sixty-eight –pounds- forty -four -pence hotel bill?! She produced her card and made the payment, hoping that Tom would never find out.

Chapter Seventeen

It was five days before Pip rang. Nikki had hoped he would have at least made sure she'd got home alright but had got used to the fact he just didn't think like she did. They flirted and giggled about their night in London. Eventually Nikki asked him about the bill for the room. Pip laughed

"Well you did say you wanted to get me something special for Christmas and as the tickets were refunded I thought you wouldn't mind"

He had no intention of paying for the room and didn't even offer to go halves.

"You could have *warned* me Pip. And I'm worried Tom may see my credit card bill. How am I to explain that?" she was worried but Pip didn't seem to care.

"I wasn't aware he took that much notice of what you did, Nik, and anyway you'd think of something." Nikki was annoyed but just thinking about their night together made her forgive him anything.

They had planned to meet up two of three times before they *actually* saw each other again. Pip had rung and cancelled last minute, the first time, giving no explanation.

The next two occasions, he just hadn't bothered to turn up. It was now nearly a month since they'd been together. Tom was away with work, the boys were at school and Pip turned up out of the blue. Nikki looked a mess. She had emptied all the kitchen cupboards and was deep cleaning.

"Stick the kettle on, Nik. On your own?" said Pip as he kissed her cheek and pushed past her into the kitchen. Although she was really pleased to see him, she couldn't help feeling a little annoyed he hadn't called first, to make sure it was convenient. She followed him into the kitchen and cleared a space on the table to put the coffee cups.

"You could have rung." she said as she filled the kettle.

"Thought I'd surprise you." he grinned and made a gesture towards his groin.

"I didn't mean *now*, I meant the last couple of times. I waited for you. You could have let me know if you weren't going to show." she said rather annoyed.

"Oooh tetchy" laughed Pip, "I'm here now, come here." he said and pulled her towards him. Nikki pulled back and continued to make the coffee.

"Oh dear, we *are* cross." teased Pip.

"Yes, I am a bit. It's not always easy to get away, Pip, but I do. I have done, whenever you've asked me to. It's not nice being stood up."

"It's not easy for me either, Nik, I'd have been there if I could, something came up." Pip stated quite matter-of –fact-ly and without sounding in anyway apologetic.

"What? What is *so* important and urgent you can't even pick up the phone?" She looked him straight in the eye as she served the coffee and put a small plate of homemade chocolate cake on the table. She had never really questioned him before, they had never argued, they had only every laughed, loved and been there for each other.

Pip's expression changed.

"Don't need this from *you*, Nik, let's just have coffee. And a cuddle would be nice?" Nikki still felt she deserved some sort of explanation. So she pushed him a little further. Pip snapped at her

"For fuck's sake, Nik, let it *go*. I'm here now."

Nikki was shocked. She had never heard him speak like that, certainly not to her anyway. She didn't deserve it. She got up and took her coffee into the living room. She stood staring out of the bay window with her hands warming round the cup. After a couple of minutes Pip came and stood beside her. She was crying.

"Don't, Nik, I'm sorry, there's been a lot going on lately. When I'm with you, I can forget all that crap." Pip put his arms round her waist. She felt the warm tingle in her tummy that took over her whole body whenever he touched her. She put down her cup, wiped her eyes on her bleach stained over-sized baggy tee shirt, took his face in her hands and softly kissed his lips.

"Tell me," she said tenderly, "*Please* Pip, talk to me. We should share everything. You always listen to me, but you tell me so little...."

"Not sure you'd want to hear it" he shrugged.

"I *do* Pip. I might be able to help" she said.

Pip faked a laugh,

"I very much doubt it." he replied.

"Try me" she said. Pip sat on the settee and held on to Nikki as she sat down next to him. She leant backwards into his chest and he wrapped his arms round her shoulders. He started to talk about Carrie. She was nineteen now and Pat had no idea where she was. She had been in contact with Pip a few times, mainly asking for money. She was the reason he had left Nikki to pay for the hotel room. She had taken advantage of her father's good nature and had practically cleared out his business account. It wasn't until Pip went to get cash from the hole in the wall on the train platform that he realized what had happened. How could he have told Nikki then? It was their special night and nothing was going to spoil that. So he chose not to say anything. But he had guessed what had happened. Carrie was now in South Africa with some bloke and pregnant for the third time. The other two children had been taken into care and she had seemed to show no regret for this at all. Nikki could hear in Pip's voice how hard it was for him to tell her all this, but there was also a sense of relief. He hadn't told anybody else, not even his wife. Pip held her tight and she listened without interruption. The way Carrie had treated both of them over the years was dreadful. Pat had done her best for her, but Carrie had never returned her love and as soon as she could she had left home. Pip had always been a soft touch - anything for an easy life. He was paying for that now.

"Why do you let her treat you like that?" asked Nikki after a long pause.

"I can't risk her upsetting everything." he replied

"Especially, my mum. I won't have her upset. She's not in the best of health and we moved her into a nursing home a couple of weeks ago. If she got to know the truth, it would kill her, Nik."

"A lot of young girls get pregnant - would it be that much of a shock? asked Nikki.

"I didn't mean *that*." Pip sounded sad he took a deep breath and said

"Carrie is my brother's daughter." he said.

"What?" Nikki turned round to look at Pip. He had started now, there was no going back. For the last twenty years he had kept this secret all to himself and thought he would never tell. But now it all came pouring out. Secrets always will, sooner or later. Nikki listened in almost disbelief. Simon was four years older than Pip, he was the apple of his mother eye and whenever the two of them had got into mischief, it was Pip who took the blame. Simon got away with *everything*. Well almost. He had got in with a group of mates whilst doing his apprenticeship for a plumbing company. There were five of them that went around together and Simon was the youngest of the group. They regularly drank and gambled away their earnings and held little regard for those around them. Pip had bailed him out on numerous occasions, lent him money and told up-teen lies to their mother to protect her. But what he was to tell Nikki next, really shocked her. Simon had been involved in, and convicted of gang rape. He had been sentenced and imprisoned for fifteen years.

"Is he out now?" interrupted Nikki.

"No, he was out after twelve but was re-arrested for affray and assault on a couple from the old gang. He insists he was stitched up. He's serving the remainder of the original sentence plus an additional three years." Nikki looked at Pip. She could see the sadness in his eyes.

"Carrie was the result of the rape" Pip went on "Pat was

the victim. He knew her, they all did. We all did. She used to work on the trade counter on the industrial estate before she left to work in the kitchen at the hotel. She had a bit of a reputation with the lads, but she didn't deserve that, no one deserves that. Anyway, *obviously*, she went to the police, Simon and the others were arrested but it was Simon who fathered Carrie. Pat was adamant about that. Once he was convicted she came to me and threatened to tell our mother unless I took responsibility for my brother actions."

"What!" Nikki almost yelled "You've gotta be kidding. Are you saying you married Pat because of Simon just so your mum wouldn't know?"

"*Please* understand Nik, it would have *killed* our mum, we are all she's got. Dad died when we were boys, I was only four, Si was eight, she worked so hard to keep us together and we never went without, but it was *really* tough for her. She *adores* Simon, it would break her heart. I couldn't bear that."

"Where does she think he is, surely she's wondered why she hasn't seen him for all these years?" Nikki was finding all of this really hard to get her head round.

"She thinks he works on the rigs; just thinks he's busy, he sends a card every birthday, Christmas and Mothering Sunday to us and I take it to her with flowers or chocolates or something and say they're from him." Pip paused for a bit,

"The thing is, he's due out next month, in time for Christmas."

"What are you going to do?"

"Honestly?" said Pip "I have absolutely no idea."

"I assume he knows about Carrie?" asked Nikki.

"Yes, but he doesn't know Carrie knows about him." replied Pip.

"Has she always known?"

"No, she and Pat had a massive row about five years ago, Carrie was starting to push the boundaries a bit; drinking, smoking staying out late, being a real bitch. I don't think I realized quite how bad it was getting. You know I was hardly ever at home and, when I was, Carrie was always sweet with me. That girl had me wrapped right round her little finger and she knew it. I just didn't see it, or chose not to. But she had grown into a very manipulative young woman. I didn't know Pat had told her about Simon until last month. Carrie had taken herself abroad and wanted money. I'd told her she wasn't getting any more until she came home and it was then she let on she knew the whole sordid truth. She blackmailed me, Nik. She said she'd tell her Granny everything about her precious Simon, if I didn't send her money" Pip hung his head.

What was he to have done?

He started to cry. And the relief was enormous. Nikki held him tight. He really needed her. She stroked his hair and let him sob. They were interrupted by the front door bell. She look at him, horrified they were about to get caught together, not that it would bother her, but that really would be the last thing *he* needed just now. The bell went again, and then a knock.

"Answer it and get rid of them." said Pip as he went into the kitchen.

"Just a parcel for next door." said Nikki as she came back in.

Pip was holding a photograph taken at the very first

'*Challenge Everyone*' camp they had been on together. He smiled at Nikki,

"That seems an awfully long time ago. Happy days eh?"

"Special days" she replied.

"I'm making a fresh coffee" said Pip, "the last one's gone cold."

Chapter Eighteen

Nikki turned thirty on the second of December. Suzanne was taking her to the theatre and out for a meal as Tom hadn't planned anything. He had left a bunch of lilies and holly in the kitchen sink for her to find when she got up. He had left early that morning for Carlisle and was going to be away for a couple of days. The card he wrote was sentimental and concluded with *all my love always, your, Tom,* which would have been lovely, if she felt he meant it. The flowers reminded her of a wreath and she left them in the sink late into the morning before she could bring herself to find a suitable vase. She thought he might just have made a bit more of an effort this year.

Charley and Harry were whispering on the landing. Nikki pretended not to hear them. They had a secret plan. Charley organized his little brother. After a few minutes of kafuffle, two angelic faces appeared at the kitchen door. Still dressed in their pyjamas and with their hair all ruffled. The brother's squealed, "Happy birthday, Mummy!" Awkwardly walking towards her, they carried a parcel, tied with a big red ribbon, between them, both clutching homemade cards.

"Grandma helped us get your present," beamed Charley "but we made the cards ourselves"

"We did-id a cake too," added Harry, "It's at Grandma's."

"That's a *surprise*." said Charley looking sternly at Harry who had given it away. Harry looked sad.

"It's a good job you told me Harry I will make sure I save some room for that later." Nikki said as she cuddled him. She couldn't bear to see him look upset. He grinned broadly at his mother. Nikki read the cards and looked at the big round ball on the front of Harrys'.

"What a beautiful sunshine." she smiled.

"It's *you* mummy." Harry grinned.

Her boys were adorable. She felt her eyes fill with tears as she read *I love you lots and lots and lots from Charley xxxxxxxxxxxx*. And the big misshaped letters where Harry had tried really hard to write *To Mummy, love from Harry*. The letters got smaller as they've curved round the shape to the card. Nikki would treasure these forever. She unwrapped the box which concealed the pink fluffy slippers which the boys had told grandma *mummy would really like*. Nikki put them on and the delight on her son's faces was magical.

After breakfast, Nikki walked the boys to school. Harry was going to start full time after Christmas and Nikki planned to return to work once he had settled. She was thinking about this as she walked back home in the winter sunshine. It was 1992. Tom had recently brought her a mobile phone that she didn't really want. It was only slightly smaller than a house brick and weighed about the same. Soon, everyone was going to have one, so Tom had said, but Nikki didn't really see the need for them. However, she had learnt how to programme a few numbers in, and at least, Pip could call her without worrying someone else might pick up. So it did have some advantages. The phone rang in her bag.

"Happy birthday, hen" came a familiar voice she hadn't heard for some time.

"Danny!" she was so surprised, "You remembered, thank you, how are you?" she asked.

"Busy as ever, I bumped into Suzanne and John the other week and promised to call you, Suze thinks you're a bit down, are you okay?" Danny replied.

"Oh, you know me, I'm alright, Danny, we must meet up and have a proper catch up." she said.

"That's partly why I was ringing," Danny went on "How are you fixed New Year? I don't suppose you fancy helping out and old friend, I need some staff at the *Railway View*?"

Nikki was flattered to be asked.

"Don't answer now" Danny went on "Let's do lunch Thursday or Friday this week, you can tell me then, my treat for your birthday."

"I'd love too, Friday's good for me." Nikki replied.

As soon as Nikki got home, the house phone rang. It was Marion and Derek singing *Happy Birthday* down the line, even though she would be seeing them later as they were babysitting. The postman delivered cards amongst the bills and junk mail and Nikki poured herself a coffee and sat down to take her time in opening them. Her mobile rang again.

"Happy birthday, darling" said Pip "is the kettle on?" Nikki's heart skipped as it always did when he rang.

"Yes." she replied.

"Well open the door then, I'm freezing my nuts off out here!" he laughed. He was already outside. She opened the door and as he stepped inside he pushed her against the wall kissing her passionately. She had barely shut the door before he started to undress her. They stumbled into the living room and frantically made love. It was brief but incredibly exciting for both of them. Spontaneous, risky sex nearly always is. Nikki loved the way he took charge. She felt completely over powered by him and that was a huge turn on. Pip stood up and pulled up his trousers.

"God, I feel better for that," he grinned "Coffee?" He helped himself and then came and sat beside her. He pulled out a small box from his pocket, opened the lid and took out the small heart shaped gold signet ring.

"I want you to wear this," he said putting it on her little finger "you're my girl Nikki. Promise me you always will be?" Nikki was stunned. He had never bought her anything other than a drink in the pub. She wanted to cry. This was probably the one most romantic thing he had every done. It was so unexpected, in all their years together she hadn't had so much as a card just from him. She loved it. It wasn't expensive or flash, but it was from him and to her, it meant everything.

"Thank you, I love you. I will treasure this, and yes, of course, I'm your girl, always" She kissed him long and hard. They were interrupted by the phone ringing.

"Let it ring." said Pip, but as the answer phone clicked in, Nikki could hear the school secretary's voice. She grabbed the phone. Charley had come down with a fever and needed to be collected from school. Pip gave Nikki a lift and carried Charley to his car.

When they got back, he waited while Nikki put Charley to bed.

"Thank you for bringing him home." Nikki said as she came back down the stairs. Pip put his arms round her,

"He'll be fine," said Pip, "but if you ever need me to help, you've only got to call. You know I will if I can."

Nikki felt so protected and it just made her love him all the more. At lunch time, Pip sat with Charley, while Nikki went and collected Harry. Harry was really excited to see Pip. He always messed about with the boys when he saw them, and when it was time for him to leave, Nikki wasn't sure if it was her or Harry, who felt the most disappointment. Before he left he promised Harry, he would try and see him again before Christmas.

Marion persuaded Nikki to go ahead with her night out but she returned early, worried about Charley. The following day Charley was covered head to toe in Chicken pox.

By Christmas, Harry had it too. Pip had kept his promise and had called in with chocolate snowmen for the boys early on Christmas Eve. This was really sweet of him and Nikki really felt he was beginning to get closer to all of them. He didn't stay long as the boys were not feeling that great. But Nikki was really grateful he had made the effort and at least she could steal a kiss and a hug before they had to spend Christmas apart. This was always a difficult time of the year. She missed him. The festivities were a little quieter than usual. Tom was home for just Christmas day and Boxing Day and took the opportunity to drink far too much and sleep a lot. As he told Nikki, this was the only break he'd get for a while and was going to make the most of it. He had taken another promotion with the bank that meant he was to be based in Europe for the next six months. He had done well and Nikki was pleased for him. She didn't mind the fact he was going to be away. He hadn't been at home much at all really since the boys came along. It was probably going to be better, if anything, as now she could stick to a routine. Tom always insisted that all he did was for the good of the family. It wasn't what Nikki believed. To her family time was the most important thing. The boys were growing so fast and Tom was missing so much. All the money in the world wouldn't buy back those precious years. He was driven by money. It was important to him that he had a good car and all the latest gadgets. The boys wanted for nothing, except for their daddy to be at home more often. Nikki had been brought up surrounded by love. Money had often been tight but neither she nor Suzanne went without. There's a lot of truth in the saying *you don't miss what you've never had* and that was evident for both Tom and Nikki but for two very different reasons.

What with the boys being poorly and Tom's departure to plan, Nikki hadn't been able to meet Pip. He hadn't rung either and she was desperate to know what had happened over Christmas with Simon coming out of prison. Eventually she called him. She heard the message, *'the mobile you are calling, has been disconnected.'* So, against her better judgement, she rang his home phone. That was disconnected too. Now she was worried. What the hell had happened?

Chapter Nineteen

The boys waved Tom off and rushed back inside the house to get ready for Grandma's. They had been cooped up for the last couple of weeks and were excited. They loved going to Marion's and Derek's. Suzanne and John were there too. They told the family over lunch that Charley and Harry were going to have twin cousins in the summer. Nikki was delighted. They *all* were and Harry asked if he could go with them to choose them. Charley surprised everyone by informing his little brother that you don't get to choose you just have to wait until the mummy gets very fat and then you get what you're given! Everyone thought this was hilarious but also very profound.

Nikki told her family that Danny had been in touch and had asked her to help out at the hotel New Years Eve. Nikki never assumed her parents would baby sit, and if they couldn't, it didn't matter. John suggested that if the boys wanted to stay over with him and Suzanne that it would be good practice for them. So that was arranged.

Nikki felt apprehensive as she walked up the steps of the *Railway View* hotel. It had been nearly nine years since she last worked there and an awful lot had happened in that time. The main reception area had been given a lick of paint and there were a few new furnishing but little else had changed. Mrs Pyke, the house-keeper, had retired and many of the casual staff Nikki had known had now moved on. Danny was the one constant and her *only* reason for going back.

New Years Eve was exhausting and, as in previous years, the party went on until the small hours. Danny and Nikki eventually sat down with a well earned cup of coffee about 4am.

"I just don't know what I would have done without you here tonight, hen." sighed Danny. Nikki could see her friend was worn out. Since Bernie had died Danny had aged a great deal. He was a little over sixty but looked much older. His hair was now completely silver. The deep smile lines were sagging a little and his eyes held a deep sadness.

"My pleasure," smiled Nikki "It's nice to be back, if only for tonight, I've missed it, well...... I've missed you, anyway." she said.

"Well, I know now is probably not the best time to ask, but would you consider coming back to me on a more permanent basis?"

Nikki had been thinking of going back to work once Harry started full time school but wasn't really considering the *Railway View*. She had completed a book- keeping course during her time at home with the children and had obtained a diploma. She rather fancied pursuing a career in accountancy.

"I don't think this is for me anymore, Danny," she said

gently, "I think my days of cleaning rooms and waitressing are gone now."

"That's not what I had in mind, hen, I need someone to pass the baton to. I have decided to go part time in the spring. It seems the more I do the more they expect and I've had enough." said Danny said.

Nikki laughed.

"You're not exactly *selling* it to me, Danny. And I don't want to work here, not without you. It just wouldn't be the same".

"I was thinking we could share a full time job" said Danny as he sat forward in his chair. "We could run the place between us, what do you think?"

"I don't know Danny. I'm too tired to think about it tonight. Let's meet up next week when the boys are back to school and talk about it then?"

"Date." smiled Danny. He looked genuinely relieved that Nikki had at least said she'd consider it and that was enough for him now.

When they did meet up, she didn't need that much persuading. She wanted to help her friend.

Harry settled quickly into full time school and Nikki started working three days a week at the *Railway View*. She had taken on the role of bookings secretary and personnel manager. Neither of which she felt practically qualified for but, as Danny pointed out, he wasn't either and she would have to learn as *he* had done, by actually *doing* the job. On her second day she drew up a list to arrange to meet with all the personnel and talk to them on a one-to-one basis. If she was going to do this job, she wanted to do it right. Most of the staff worked part time or casual and it was her intention to get to know all of them and make them feel valued. Danny had been good at this and it had made such a difference to her in the past. Within the first month she had met with all of them. All accept one, Pat.

Pat had been off work since just before Christmas. She was due back on Monday and it was Nikki's job to conduct the return to work interview. She was dreading it, but at least she might find out if Pip was ok.

Pat knocked on the door of the small office behind the reception desk

"Oh my gawd," she practically shouted "what you doing back 'ere?" she asked Nikki.

"I'm the personnel manager now." replied Nikki feeling ever so slightly smug, "Please take a seat. Thank you for coming in to see me today." she went on "I understand you have been away for the past nine weeks?" Nikki was very professional and Pat sat down and clutched her handbag into her lap. She looked tired and for a moment Nikki felt a little sorry for her. That soon passed. After all, this was the woman who prevented her being with the man she loved. "Would you like to tell me, in your own words, why you have been away? I can find no record of sickness certificates or indeed application for holiday." Nikki said as she opened Pat's file. Pat fidgeted in the chair.

"Personal reasons." was her sharp reply.

"You're going to have to elaborate on that" insisted Nikki "I can't use that as a justifiable explanation for your absence."

Pat glanced round the room and shuffled her feet.

"I'm back now," she said "are you going to let me start work or not?" Nikki raised her eyebrows "I don't think you realize the seriousness of the situation," said Nikki "I can't let you walk back in without completing this interview satisfactorily and for that I need you to give me some answers."

Pat stood up. There was no way she was going to tell Nikki anything. She leant in towards Nikki's face.

"Mind your own fucking business." she said, "And you can stick this shit job, where the sun don't shine. Now that's given you something to write in your little file ain't it?" And with that she walked out the room.

Nikki was stunned. She didn't quite know what to do. As far as the job was concerned she needed to complete the appropriate forms, to close Pat's file. But for herself, she was still none the wiser as to what had happened to Pip. She just needed to know if he was ok. Then she had an overwhelming fear that maybe somehow, Pat knew about her and Pip. Oh, God, what if she did? What if she had found out and had done something dreadful to him? That would explain why she hadn't heard from him. Nikki began to get more than a little anxious. She was going to have to find out, but how? Nikki picked up the phone to call Danny. She explained the meeting with Pat. Danny was relieved she had walked out as it saved them having to sack her. Although Danny knew about Pip and Nikki's relationship, Nikki hadn't told him how close they had become. She had decided it was much safer to keep things to herself. So when he asked if she still saw Pip, she just said that they hadn't seen each other in a while, which was true, but led Danny to believe that things had really cooled off between them. She did, however, say she was concerned for him, without giving any reason why, other than that Pat seemed angry and aggressive and it was then that Danny suggested she visited them, for her own piece of mind.

"Oh, I'll just turn up, shall I?" questioned Nikki, "Hello Pat, how are you? Thought I'd just drop by to see if you were ok after telling me to mind my own fucking business and also to see if you've done your husband in?" she added sarcastically. Danny thought for a bit.

"I see your point, hen. But you and Pip have been friends for years, he might be glad to see you?"

Danny was right, it wasn't going to be easy but Nikki had to know if Pip was alright. Her shift finished at 5pm. Marion had collected the boys from school earlier and was giving them their tea at her house. Nikki rang her to let her know something had come up and she was going to be an hour late. Marion said that it would be alright on this occasion but she wasn't to make a habit of it. Nikki knew not to push her luck with her parents. Neither of them had wanted her to return to work. She didn't *need* to on the money Tom earned enough for the family and as far as they were concerned, her job was at home with her boys. Nikki could see their point of view but she wanted her own money, and not to be totally financially dependent on Tom. Plus she needed more in her life now that both the boys were at full time school.

Nikki left the hotel and drove to Pip's house. She had only been there a couple of times before and didn't feel at all comfortable with what she was doing. She could see the living room light on as she approached the front door. Taking a deep breath she rang the bell.

"You get it." she heard Pat shout and within a couple

of minutes Pip opened the door. His sad, tired face broke into a smile

"Hello. This is a nice surprise. Business, or pleasure? He winked before hastily adding that Pat was in the bathroom and would be down in a minute.

"God, Pip, you look awful. Are you okay? Why haven't you rung? I've been worried sick and your phones disconnected." she whispered

"Long story, I can't talk now" Pip answered as Pat came down the stairs towards the front door. "Oh, what do you want?" she asked Nikki.

"I've come to see if you're okay?" Nikki replied.

"Come in. Have you got time for a cup of tea?" Pip said stepping back from the door. It was an interesting scenario, none of them knew exactly what the other two knew and Nikki was going to have to tread very carefully.

Pip showed her into the lounge and went to put the kettle on. Pat sat down opposite Nikki. Neither woman knew quite what to say. So Nikki started with

"We've known each other a long time Pat. You and Pip are friends. I didn't want what happened earlier to spoil that".

"Ha" scoffed Pat, "bit late for that" Pip brought the tea through. The room fell silent. Pat slurped at her tea and then looking straight at Nikki said.

"Mrs Denton has come to offer me my job back, isn't that right?" Nikki didn't know what to say and before she *could* say anything, Pip responded with "Oh that is good news, thank you, Nikki, Pat said you had to let her go earlier? We could really do with the money right now, as I'm not able to work at the moment."

What? She hadn't come to do *anything* of the sort! Why wasn't he able to work?

"Oh I'm sorry to hear that Pip. What's the matter?" she asked.

"Told you she was a nosey bitch." said Pat.

Pip looked at Nikki, this was so uncomfortable, but he didn't tell his wife not to be rude and that annoyed Nikki.

"Sorry, none of my business." said Nikki.

"That's okay, had a bit of an accident, with a chisel, just before Christmas" said Pip "Went right up under my rib and punctured a lung."

Nikki felt the colour drain from her cheeks. She wanted to hug him and tell him she'd look after him. But how could she?

"Should be okay in a couple of weeks," Pip went on "but in the mean time, if Pat's working, that's going to help."

What could she do? Danny had wanted Pat gone for some time. Pip needed Pat to be working. Nikki found herself asking Pat to start back the following week, albeit on less hours.

Pat showed Nikki to the door. She needed to get back for the boys. She was annoyed with herself, angry with Pat and sad for Pip. Why hadn't he told her? Something wasn't right. She needed to talk to him, alone, just the two of them. She just wanted to be with him. She had missed him and today made that worse.

Danny had taken a bit of persuading as far as the re-employment of Pat went, but he loved having Nikki back and agreed to give Pat one last chance. He could see Nikki wanted to help Pip and how worried she was for him. He had tried to lighten the situation by joking, perhaps Pip had tried to do away with Pat so he could be with her and it had all gone wrong. The joke was in bad taste and Nikki didn't find it funny. It just worried her even more.

Pat turned up for work on the following Monday as if nothing had happened and although Nikki felt she was owed an apology - or at least a thank you - she got neither. Thursday was going to be the first opportunity for Nikki to contact Pip. Pat would be at work and Nikki wasn't. She planned to visit him.

Pip opened the door and quickly ushered Nikki inside, he didn't want her to be seen. But there was no hug or even a kiss on the cheek. Pip was very pale and distant. Something was definitely wrong.

Chapter Twenty

Nikki offered to make the coffee and brought it through to the lounge. Pip was standing staring out of the window.

"I'm sorry Nikki but I don't think we should see each other anymore," he said continuing to stare straight ahead and making no attempt to look at her. Nikki felt a pain go through her and felt she could hardly breathe. But rather than shout at him or demand an explanation, she calmly sat down and took a sip from her coffee mug.

"Did you hear me?" asked Pip. "Leave, Nik, just leave".

From where she was sitting she could see a tear roll down his cheek.

"I heard you" she replied gently "And if I thought you meant it I'd go. But you don't. You just want to protect me from something and you need to tell me what that is. Darling, I'm not going anywhere, I promised you years ago I'd always be yours and just because we didn't actually say any marriage vows, -well, not to each other anyway - I meant to love you forever, through the good times and the bad. Whatever's happened, Pip, I want to help you. And you can start by telling me the truth about the chisel...."

"Bugger, you can nag." said Pip as he sat down beside her and a slight smile came across his face.

"It's a real mess, Nik, I don't want to involve you. To be honest I think my heads going to burst with all that's going on. And having an affair is the last thing I need right now." Nikki glared at him.

"Then stop thinking of us as *an affair*. We're so much more than that and you *know* it. I'm your best friend and confidante too." she said firmly.

"Fair play." smiled Pip, "As long as you don't try and seduce me while you're being *my friend*, I don't think I could manage it at the moment." That was more like her Pip and Nikki kissed his cheek.

"That's all you're getting..... for now." she smiled.

Pip took his coffee and sat in the arm chair across the room. Nikki could see that he was finding it hard to sit comfortably, he was obviously in pain. They sat quietly and had almost finished their coffee before Pip finally started to speak.

"Simon came out of prison just before Christmas. He turned up here Christmas Eve. He had no-where else to go Nik, what was I supposed to do? He's my brother. Pat was shopping when he arrived and he persuaded me we could get her to agree to let him stay if only for a few days. It wasn't going to be easy to find anywhere else over the holiday period" Pip looked so sad as he spoke. Nikki asked.

"Doesn't the prison provide a halfway house or something for ex- cons when they first get out?"

"Not if they are told they have family to go to." said Pip. "Bloody ridiculous, he told them he could live with his brother. He failed to mention that his brother had married his victim. They would never have allowed that".

"You'd think they'd check it out, wouldn't you?" asked Nikki.

"Well, we'd like to think so but I think we've all watched far too many TV cop shows, real life isn't like that Nik. They don't seem to give a shit about anyone. Once Simon had served his time, he was no longer their responsibility and it was all too long ago for the so called 'victim support' to take any interest. So what was I to do? I let him into the kitchen and made him something to eat. He wanted to visit mum so we were making plans, when Pat came home."

Pip's face was grey and expressionless as he told Nikki what happened next. "She bundled the shopping into the hall and called through to me to give her a hand. Before I could get up Simon walked up the hallway towards her. *'Hello Pat'*, he said, calm as you like, *'let me help you with that, it's the least I can do.'* I can't describe the look on her face Nik and for the first time in many years I just wanted to protect her. She dropped the bags she was holding and screamed at me *'get that* bastard out of our house'. I tried to get past Simon, to get to Pat, but he moved towards her telling her to *'let bygones be bygones'*. Like he'd nicked her bike or something. My tool belt was on the foot of the stairs, I'd left it there after putting the Christmas tree in one of them bases, I'd needed to trim it down a bit and screw it in. I was about to put it back in the van, when Simon had rung the doorbell. Anyway, Pat grabbed the chisel and pointed it at Simon. *Get out, get out, get out,* she screamed and screamed at him. I tried to get between them to sort things out and calm her down, but she lunged towards him, lost her footing, fell over the shopping and I caught the full force."

"Oh my God, Pip, she could have *killed* you!" Nikki's eyes welled up, "What happened next?"

"It was all a bit of a blur really. I couldn't breathe properly, and fell to the floor. Pat shouted at Simon' *look at what you've done, you'll pay for this'*. She must have been in shock, she made no attempt to help me and God only knows where I'd be now, if Simon hadn't pushed her out of the way. He grabbed the phone and called an ambulance. Pat just sat on the stairs and watched as Simon packed a tea towel round the chisel and told me not to pull it out." Pip half laughed

"Prison taught him something. He'd learnt first aid. Apparently he saved my life by leaving that sticking out of me. So Christmas Eve was spent with me in hospital. Simon was in a cell and Pat being comforted by a policewoman, for most of the evening. She'd told them, Simon stabbed me."

"But he didn't, Pip, she did. You should tell them the truth?" said Nikki.

"How's that going to help anyone, Nik? It was an accident. She didn't stab me intentionally, she had had an awful shock, I should never have let him in."

Pip got up and took the mugs into the kitchen. Nikki followed him.

"Where is Simon now?" she asked. Pip started to run the taps.

"Awaiting trial" he replied without looking up.

"What for? Nikki looked confuse, "You don't mean she's saying he stabbed you on *purpose,* Pip?" Nikki was finding this all a little hard to take in.

"Look, Nik, I told you from the start, I don't want

you involved in any of this. I have to stick by Pat, she see's getting Simon sent down again, as her chance for revenge, I owe her that."

"Bollocks Pip." said Nikki, "You owe her nothing. And if the truth comes out, you'll be in trouble too. *Please* don't do this, Pip."

"It's too late, Nik, I already have. And there's something else......," Pip took a deep breath, "Carrie's coming home tomorrow." Pip looked up at the ceiling. "I can hardly wait," he said sarcastically "She's about all I need right now."

He walked over to Nikki.

"I know this is a big ask, but *please*, try not to worry about me. This is a huge mess but it'll get sorted out. The best way you can help me is to stay away for a while. *Please*, Nik?"

He took her hand and turned the ring on her finger he had given her for her birthday.

"Remember sweetheart, we're together forever, even when we're apart for a while." he gently kissed her lips and she promised to do as he asked. She loved him so much, but there was nothing more she could do to help him until he asked her too.

It was nearly six months before she saw him again.

Chapter Twenty One

Charley and Harry bounced on the end of Nikki's bed.

"Wake up Mummy," they beamed "we're going to Winnies' house."

Winnie was a lifelong friend of Marion's, and all through her life, Nikki, Suzanne and their parents had spent their summers at her holiday cottage. Winnie was in her eighties now and lived in an adjoining annexe. She loved to see the children and was looking forward to it as much as they were. Tom had taken a few days off and was going with them for at least part of the week and Marion and Derek were going to join Nikki and the boys for the rest of the time.

Nikki hugged her boys tight.

"Better get a wiggle on then." This was one of Danny's old sayings and it made the boys laugh. They stuck out their bottoms and wiggled across the bedroom. Nikki laughed. She was so looking forward to this week away. Work had become demanding and she needed this holiday. The cottage was on the North Norfolk coast, away from everything. It was quaint and old fashioned. There as an old Roberts radio (which Tom commented must be worth a bit) but no television. Consequently, even rainy days, were fun days. They always found plenty to do. Nikki loved it there.

By the Wednesday, Tom had returned to London. He worked there most of the time now. The few days he had spent with the boys had been wonderful, for *them* anyway. But it had also made Nikki realise, that, apart from Charley and Harry, they had very little in common. He rarely spoke to Nikki and wasn't interested in her conversation. They had grown apart. But in a strange way, it seemed to suit them both. Although they were married, they had become very separate people. Friday was the last full day of their holiday. Marion packed up a picnic and Derek had found all the old crabbing lines in the run down out house. Nikki showed Charley and Harry the stones Suzanne and she had found years earlier.

"Granddad used to take us onto the beach and we would look for stones with holes in them, we needed them to tie onto the crab line." she told them. They were such happy days but Nikki hadn't been on the beach looking for stones for over twenty years. They had stopped going when her legs had started to need surgery. It wasn't until now that she realized just how much she'd missed it. Derek was in his element. He walked along the beach with the boys getting them to collect more stones, before joining Marion and Nikki on Cromer Pier. They had got all the lines and buckets ready for Charley and Harry but it was obvious that Derek was going to prove difficult to beat in the competition that followed.

"Derek," called Marion "Harry can hardly see around you, let him pull the line up himself." Harry's little face lit up as the biggest crab of the day clung on to his line. He pulled it slowly up to the pier rails, as instructed by his Granddad. When it was less than a foot away from his reach, he realised that he didn't really like the look of this creature and dropped the line.

"Harry!" shouted Derek "What'd you do that for? You'd got the winner there son."

Harry ran over to Nikki and buried his little blonde head in her jeans. He was crying. Nikki picked him up and hugged him. She looked at her dad.

"It's alright, Harry" she said "You just wanted to let Granddad win didn't you, so he wouldn't sulk." Harry nodded and smiled at his mum through his tear stained cheeks.

"I let you win, Granddad" he shouted.

"Come on, Harry," said Marion, "let's get your hands washed and we can get everyone an ice cream. How does that sound?"

Nikki was left sitting, on her own, for a short while. She looked far into the distance along the beach and could see a couple walking with their arms around each other. This was the only thing that was missing from her life. She wanted someone to walk along the beach with like that. She wanted to spend romantic evenings with someone she loved. She wanted to be with Pip. She always had. Thinking about him made her feel sad. She had missed him over the past few months. What was she going to do? She couldn't go on the way she was. Tom was already a part time Dad. So would getting divorced from him make much difference? Marion and Derek wouldn't approve. How would it affect the boys? No, this was silly. It's just a dream. Get real Nikki, she told herself. Pip isn't going to leave Pat. Think of all the lives you'd ruin. You should be grateful for what you have. She was just being selfish. She turned round to see Charley walking towards her slowly and carefully carrying the bucket of crabs. The concentration on his face was there for all to see, as he proudly showed off the thirty six tiny crabs they had caught.

"Granddad put his in my bucket Mummy. He said mine would be lonely." said Charley.

"Why? Did you only catch one? Nikki asked.

"No, Granddad only had three. We had to put them together so we could call it a draw." said Charley looking confused "And if you're in a draw, you get a bag of two pence's for the slot machines" he added, smiling.

"Is that right?" said Nikki looking at her father "I seem to remember I always used to draw with Granddad too, Charley."

Derek winked at her.

The holiday had been wonderful and over all too quickly. The boy's suntanned faces looked angelic as they both slept most of the journey home. Derek helped Nikki carry them up to their beds. They had spent most of the day on the beach before packing up to come home. Nikki was so grateful that she had Marion and Derek and she told them so as she hugged them before they drove back to their own home

Chapter Twenty Two

It was only because Harry and Charley had been jumping on the bunk beds that Nikki found she had a genuine excuse to ring Pip. The slats had broken and although she could probably have repaired them herself, or had Derek known, he would certainly have offered to help. But this was the first chance she had had in a long time to contact Pip. She dialled the number. It was an answering machine, so she hung up. Why? This was silly. So she rang again. She listened to the message and after the beep said, "Hi Philip, it's Nikki. Would you be able to do a bit of carpentry at my house? Please could you ring me? Thank you bye........ Oh it's Nikki by the way, did I say that? It's the bunk beds, the boys have broken the slats. Please could you ring me? Oh, I think I said that too, I'm waffling, sorry, thank you. Bye"

She put the phone down. What was she doing? She felt so nervous. She'd babbled and must have sounded so stupid and she just knew Pat would hear it and she wished she hadn't bothered. But the phone rang almost immediately.

"Are you at home now Nik?" Pip's voice sounded husk and she felt her heart pound

"Yes" she replied "Are you on your own?" he went on

"Yes" she said

"Give me ten minutes, see you soon." and he put the phone down. Nikki felt like a school girl. She hadn't seen him for six months, it seemed a lot longer and she was genuinely excited, so much so she felt sick. She opened the door and let him in. They looked at each other for the briefest of seconds before they fell into each other's arms, kissing with such intensity that they could barely breathe. Pip started to undo his trousers.

"Stop." said Nikki, "I can't Pip, the boys will be back soon with Mum. They've just walked down to the shop."

"Oh," said Pip "when I asked if you were on your own...."

"You didn't give me the chance to say much else." she laughed

"Come in the kitchen, I'll put the kettle on, they'll all love to see you." she took his hand and led him into the kitchen and they kissed and cuddled until the kettle boiled and the front door opened.

"We're back" called Marion. Pip opened the kitchen door.

"Hello all" he announced cheerily and for the first time in a very long time he sounded like the old Pip.

"Pip!" shouted Charley and ran over to him and hugged his waist.

"Wow, look at *you* Charley, you've got so tall. How old are you now, twenty?" he teased.

"No silly I'm *eight*." Charley replied.

"So, Harry how have you been? Last time I saw you, you were rather poorly" said Pip ruffling his hair.

"I'm fine and not spotty now." Harry grinned. Pip sat

on the sofa and both boys immediately jumped on him. Pip yelped and called for help, in a jokey way, but Nikki was worried they had hurt his wound.

"Be careful" she said, the concern evident in her voice.

"They're ok, Nik, I'm fine now! Pip assured her.

"How have you been Marion?" asked Pip as Nikki brought the coffee through.

"Oh we're fine, thank you, Philip. I can't remember when we last saw you. You really must come and have a coffee with Derek and I sometime. He'd love to see you." said Marion.

"I'd like that, thank you" replied Pip. Nikki smiled to herself. We'd make a lovely family, she thought. Pip drank most of his coffee and then turned to the boys.

"Right you two. Come here." he said in a stern voice that made them look more than a little worried. They both stood up straight, in front of him.

"Is it right, that you two are now so big and heavy that you have broken your beds?"

The two boys looked at each other, if they said they'd been jumping on them they might be in trouble, so it was Harry who said,

"Charley's bigger than *me*."

Charley stared at him and so as not to take all the blame himself said in his defence, "I'm a heavy sleeper."

Marion and Nikki laughed out loud. Pip tried not to laugh and the boys didn't realise what was funny.

"Well," said Pip, "If that's the case you'd better show me the damage. I may well need two young boys to help me. Do you know anyone?"

Charley lead the way up the stairs and Harry quickly followed.

"*We* can help you Pip we are really good at hammers, Granddad told me"

"Well if your Granddad recommends you, you've got the job." laughed Pip.

Marion and Nikki left the boys to it and washed up in the kitchen,

"That's good of Philip to help you out Nikki. Your father could have done it."

Nikki had wondered before if Marion had ever suspected there was anything more between her and Pip than just friendship -women often pick up on these things- but if she had, she never asked and she was never going to. Nikki could never tell her. The risk of breaking up the family would be too much. She didn't want to do anything to upset her parents. Anyway, this relationship with Pip wasn't going anywhere, so what was the point. So she replied with

"He offered Mum, and I haven't seen him for ages, I miss the old days of the camps and everyone together, it's nice to catch up."

"The boys seem to love him. He's a lovely chap Nikki" said Marion.

This was odd, and Nikki smiled to herself, it was an innocent remark but she was really pleased her Mum had noticed. Either that or she suspected there *was* more to their relationship than just friends and wanted to give Nikki the chance to say something.

"I think they miss having their Dad around." said Nikki. "Tom's going to be home soon, Mum, he only found out at the beginning of the week. There's to be a bit of a reshuffle at the bank and he will be based closer to home from now on. He'll be home a lot more than he's ever been. So as from September, we should at *last*, have some kind of normal family life."

Pip came into the kitchen with the boys just as Marion was about to reply. Nikki interrupted her

"But I haven't said anything yet as it all needs to be confirmed." she nodded towards the boys and Marion realized they didn't know. The truth was Nikki wanted to tell Pip when they were on their own. She wondered how he was going to take it. Although they didn't see each other that often, Pip always saw Nikki as *his*. Tom was just someone who turned up once in a while to see the children, but he wasn't a threat to his and Nikki's relationship, and she wanted to assure him, that this wouldn't change that.

"I'm going to have to get some replacement slats for the bunks Nik, Charley informs me they can manage tonight as long as I come back tomorrow." He added, "If that's ok with you? I'll see you about eight"?

"Thank you Pip, that'll be fine, so you two better be up and dressed ready to help Pip." Nikki said.

"We will." they promised.

Pip was as good as his word and the next day he repaired the boy's beds. He also arranged with Nikki to build a playhouse in the garden in time for Charley's birthday the following month. Nikki told Marion about the plan and she offered to have the boys for the weekend. Pip knew what he was doing. This was going to be the last chance for him and Nikki to be alone together for a while, especially now Tom was coming back.

The boys persuaded Pip into the garden for a game of

catch with Charley's rugby ball. It was full size, hard and heavy and Harry couldn't catch it. But it didn't stop him trying. He laughed all the time and his determination to keep trying was a credit to him. Pip was great with the boys. Nikki watched them through the kitchen window as she poured the coffee and made milkshakes. How she wished it could always be like this.

After the drinks the children went back outside to play. It was the first chance Pip and Nikki had the chance to talk, alone. They had been chatting and laughing together and stealing the

occasional kiss when Nikki said, "I've been wanting to ask you what happened with Simon. It's been six months since Pat stabbed you, and I haven't been able to ask *her* anything."

Pip's mood changed.

"Not much to tell really" he shrugged, "It was pretty much his word against hers, so he was released without charge, bound over for eighteen months and that was that. He's moved near Ipswich, now. We've got a cousin there who's putting him up while he gets back on his feet. He seems ok."

Nikki was stunned.

"Is that it? She stabbed you, Pip. And she lied. Are you just going to forget about that?"

"Look Nik, what's done, is done. I'm ok, Simon's moved and we're pretty much back to how things were. Let's just leave it like that." He walked over to the window. Neither of them spoke for a while.

"You've got two smashing lads there, Nik" he said trying to change the subject. Nikki was reluctant to push Pip when he was avoiding things he didn't want to answer, but she had waited long enough and felt she had the right to know.

"Thank you," she said "I know. I'm lucky and they *really* like *you*, Pip" she stood behind him and put her arms round his waist then she asked.

"Why didn't you defend Simon"? Pip just carried on watching the boys and softly replied

"I couldn't make her take the blame, Nik, not after everything we've been through, it wouldn't have been fair. It would have *finished* us."

Nikki moved away from him and sat at the table. She felt *really* hurt. Surely that would have been a good thing? After all, wasn't Pat the only reason that she and Pip weren't together?

"Do you still love me, Pip?" she said quietly.

"Of course I do. You know I do, what ever made you say that? He half laughed as he sat down next to her.

"*Do* I?" she said.

"Oh come *on*, Nik. That's not fair. You knew right from the start we could never be together full time"

It was true, she did know. But as the years had passed, she had never stopped hoping that one day, thing's would change.

"I know. Sorry, I just want you all to myself. That's all." she sniffed as she wiped a tear away. "Did Carrie come home?" she asked.

"Yes, briefly. She's moved to Ipswich too" said Pip, "Don't ask. Long story but she's out of my hair at last and I'm grateful for that at least."

There was so much Nikki wanted to ask but Pip didn't give her the chance.

"I'm sorry, love, I'm going to have to make a move". I've got a job on over at the recreation ground -vandalism in the pavilion - I promised to get there by, well, by now really" he opened the back door

"Bye, boys. Be good for your Mum" he called out.

"See you Saturday week, I should get the playhouse done in a day, unless of course I get distracted" he winked at her as they walked to the front door.

"See you then." she said, just before he kissed her passionately.

"I'll call you in the week" he called out as he put the tools back in his van. Whatever he said to her, whatever he did or didn't do, come to that, as soon as she saw him, or he kissed her or even just a wink, Nikki melted and would forgive him anything. How else would their relationship have lasted this long? He was living his life, just as he wanted to and Nikki, well, she would rather be part of it on his terms, than not at all. Even though it made her sad far more often than it made her happy. She wasn't comfortable with the conversation they had just had. Something wasn't right, she could sense it. But Pip had no reason to lie to her and she knew better than to push him. She'd missed him, and in two weeks time she was going to make the most of him. If only for a day.

Most of the playhouse was completed by lunchtime. Nikki had worked alongside Pip all morning and had enjoyed every minute of it.

"I'll come back tomorrow and finish off, if that's ok?" Pip said. They had just opened ice cold lagers from the fridge and enjoyed the sandwiches Nikki had made for them to share.

"Oh, have you got to go?" asked Nikki. Pip looked at her and laughed

"No, but I can think of a much better way we can spend this afternoon." he said and reached over to take her hand. They were barely dressed by the time they reached her bedroom. It had been such a long time since they had enjoyed each other's bodies. The sex was frantic and urgent, the first time, but they took their time for the next few hours that followed.

The house was quiet when Pip left, Nikki couldn't remember a time since having the boys that she had been on her own all night. She wished Pip could have stayed, but that wasn't possible. She played an old tape she compiled years earlier and hadn't listened to for ages, poured herself a large white wine and lay in a deep bubble bath. This was heaven. She thought about the afternoon, it had been a perfect day. She thought deeply about a lot of things. Mainly, Pip. And the fact that Tom would soon be at home, to stay.

For the first time in a long time she felt guilty. Tom had provided well for her and the boys. She knew he loved Charley and Harry and cared for her too. Really they had the perfect life. If only she could love him.

She did. She did love him, in a way, maybe not like she loved Pip. She cared for him but she was going to have to try an awful lot harder if it was going to work. All Pip really wanted her for was sex. She knew that, deep down and the more wine she drank the more she knew that to be true. So that night, she made a decision. Tomorrow she would tell Pip that she wouldn't be able to see him when Tom got back.

She couldn't. Tom deserved *better*. Pip would be ok about it. He wouldn't contact her. It was nearly *always* her that got in touch first anyway.

It would be easy. If she didn't see him, she could get on with her life with Tom. No one need ever know she and Pip had been lovers and no one would get hurt. She poured the last of the wine into her glass as she got out of the bath. The tape played the Seekers *The Carnival Is Over* and she listened intently to the lyrics for the first time. How ironic, she thought to herself, it's a sign. She could do this. She had to make it work with Tom because her beautiful children deserved it. She just had to be determined. Tomorrow she would finish her relationship with Pip. It was for the best, for everyone.

Nikki dried her hair and fell into bed. The wine had done what she wanted it to do. The lyrics went round and round in her head *'this will be our last goodbye, though the carnival is over, I will love you 'til I die'* She knew she would always love Pip but she had made her mind up.

It didn't mean she didn't cry herself to sleep though.

Chapter Twenty Three

Pip had made a fantastic job of the playhouse. Marion and Derek were bringing the boys back in time for them all to share Sunday lunch. Pip came in from the garden

"Something smells good." he said and kissed Nikki's neck. She turned and kissed his cheek. His strong arms held her tight and he started to put his hand inside her top.

"Stop, Pip, we *can't*, Mum will be here soon, it's not worth the risk." she said

"Charming," shrugged Pip "So I'm not worth it now?" he teased.

"I didn't mean that, it would be silly to risk getting caught now, that's all" said Nikki

"Why is now any different? he asked. "I thought that was always part of the thrill?" he grinned. There was never going to be a good time for Nikki to say what she needed to say and if she didn't say it now, she never would.

"I love you Pip, you know I do." she said. Pip interrupted

"I kind of got that impression, especially after yesterday." he smiled

"Please, *please* let me finish" she went on "We had a

wonderful day yesterday, Pip – perfect- but I want all our days to be like that. I want to be happy *everyday*, but I can't, not without you. And because of you I can't be happy with Tom either." She looked down at the vegetables she was boiling on the stove.

"You've always known the situation, Nik, I can't *leave* Pat, I told you that from the start." he replied.

"Yes you did. But I was young then and everything you told me I just accepted. But we've been together nearly twenty years now and, I'm sorry, Pip, I just don't know what else to do. I really can't see any reason for you not to leave her. Carries' left home, you don't love Pat - or you say you don't - but you *must* do. You'd be wonderful with the boys, they adore you and I, well I would make you so happy. Every day I would make you happy....." Nikki could feel her eyes started to well up. "It's taken me along time but I realize that you just don't love me enough do you?" she said as she looked him straight in the eyes.

"You deserve so much better." he said softly. "I do love you, Nikki but you've got your life with Tom."

This wasn't really the answer Nikki wanted to hear. She wanted him to fight for her.

But he didn't.

There it was, she'd said it and he hadn't put up any resistance. That said it all, didn't it?

The door bell rang over and over and two very excited little boys flew into the house.

"We're home, Mummy" squealed Charley and Harry.

"Stay there a minute, don't come in the kitchen," said Nikki as she wiped the tears from her cheeks. "I've got a surprise for you".

Pip stuck his head round the door

"Hooray" shouted Harry "It's Pip!" All the adults laughed.

"Well, yes it is" said Marion, "But I think Mummy has another surprise" The boys shut their eyes tight. Pip picked Harry up and Nikki took Charley's hand and led everyone out into the garden.

"Keep your eyes shut tight" Pip told them "We can all count to three and then open our eyes together ready? One, two..... three......."

The look of delight on the boy's faces was priceless.

"Wow!" yelled Charley, as he ran to look inside. Harry just stared.

"Can we *keep* it Pip?" he asked. Pip ruffled his hair and stood him down

"Yes, you can keep it,...... yours forever." he said and looked at Nikki. Nikki felt uncomfortable. "You staying for lunch Philip?" asked Marion.

"Afraid not, Mrs E." replied Pip, "wife's expecting me." He shook Derek's hand and promised catch up with him soon.

"Bye bye, boys. Enjoy your new house." Pip shouted.

"It's brilliant, Pip. Thank you" shouted Charley. Harry didn't shout. Harry ran over to Pip, hugged his leg and kissed his jeans before running back to the playhouse laughing. Nikki followed Pip through the house to see him out. She helped him put the tools back in his van. "They love it. Thank you so much, Pip." said Nikki.

"My pleasure." smiled Pip. They looked at each other and Nikki wanted to take back all she had said that morning. But she said nothing.

"See you sometime?" said Pip as he got into the van. He started the engine, and pulled away from the drive without looking back. Nikki could feel her heart breaking. When? When would she see him? Not for a long time.

Chapter Twenty Four

For the next few years the Denton family home functioned much as any other normal family Tom took more of a share in looking after the boys which made Nikki's working life that much easier. She attended a number of training courses, took some exams and decided to pursue a career in personnel management. She eventually left the hotel chain and took a promotion with a large retail company. Leaving the *Railway View* was tinged with a little sadness as she had spent so many happy times there. But it had all changed now. Danny had long since retired, the staff were constantly changing and even Pat had left to work in a cafe. Staying with the company would have meant changing hotels and that would have involved either a long commute each day or moving. Neither of these options appealed and she didn't even discuss it with Tom. She just bided her time until something came up closer to home. Charley and Harry were doing well at school. Charley had started secondary school the previous September and excelled at mathematics and science. He had also made the rugby team, which had pleased him no end. Harry was not so academic and spent a lot of his spare time with his Granddad. They were like peas in a pod. Most weekends Harry and Derek would be making something in Derek's shed and Harry had developed some real skills for carpentry. To all intents and purposes they were the ideal family.

Nikki often thought about Pip but she kept her promise to herself and made no attempt to contact him. Pip didn't try to get in touch with her, either. She knew he wouldn't. All she had to do was stay away from him. She just had to make sure, she didn't see him. The feelings she got when she did, would be too hard to ignore. It was easy enough to do really. They didn't move in the same circles anymore. While the boys still needed baby-sitting, Nikki would offer to stay at home and let Tom go to any parties, Pip might be at. They had become few and far between as most of the group from the old days had moved away and grown apart. Nikki knew Pip now had little to do with the camps and charity he had helped to set up all that time ago although he still met up with some of them from time to time. Tom and Nikki were invited to a reunion weekend. Nikki thought Tom would jump at the chance to go and that would have been difficult to get out of. She was relieved when it was Tom who said that they had very little in common with the old crowd now and he didn't see the point. Nikki actually thought this made Tom seem a real snob. He obviously thought they were better than *slumming* it in a field for the weekend and that annoyed Nikki. Part of her wanted to go just to prove a point, it would have been great. The boys would have loved it, but she just couldn't risk seeing Pip. She had missed him too much. The slightest smile from him would put her right back to square one and she couldn't risk that. Not while her boys still needed her anyway.

But some things just can't be avoided.

It was late March, 1999. Tom had taken the boys fishing with his father, something they very rarely did. Charley had wanted to stay with Nikki but he spent far too much time in the house. She thought the fresh air would do him good and had insisted he'd go. They left earlier that Saturday morning and after waving them off, Nikki took her coffee up to the bathroom for a long soak in the bath. She lay there smiling to herself. A couple of years ago she would have been straight on the phone letting Pip know she had the house to herself. Thinking of him made her feel happy. After all, they'd had some good times, some *really* good times and where was the harm in reliving them, if only in her head? She was in her bedroom drying her hair when the phone rang.

"Hi, Nikki? It's me." came the voice.

Pip's voice.

Nikki sat on the bed "Spooky." she laughed "I was just thinking about you. How have you been?"

"Ok," Pip replied, "Look, is Tom there?" he asked.

"No, he's taken the boys fishing all day, why?" Nikki felt herself beginning to get flirtatious, she couldn't help herself. He always had that effect on her.

"Are you on your own then?" Pip asked.

"Yes....Why?... What did you have in mind?" she whispered.

"I just need to see you, Nik, put the kettle on, see you in ten." he said and hung up. Nikki quickly got dressed and went down stairs. She hadn't planned this. But she'd be fine.

Don't let him get to you. You can just be friends. She told herself. But she was pleased it was him who had given in first and her tummy was turning cartwheels by the time he rang the bell. She opened the door."

Hi," she beamed, "this is a nice surprise."

Pip followed her through to the kitchen.

"Sit down, Nik, I'll pour" he said.

Something was wrong, she could sense it.

"Whatever's the matter, Pip?" she asked.

"I didn't want to tell you over the phone, not if you were on your own, I'm sorry Nik, there's no easy way to say it so I'll just say it. Danny's died" Pip told her. Nikki stared at him. Her mind had been racing with the thought of just seeing Pip again but what he had just told her had knocked her for six. She sat motionless staring at the floor.

"What? When?" she asked, sounding like a little girl.

"Tuesday sometime. Probably. The woman who cleaned for him found him Wednesday morning. I didn't want you to read it in the paper or something. I bumped into the landlord of the *Locomotive,* purely by chance at the petrol station yesterday. He wanted your number. I said I'd tell you. He still wants to contact you though, Nik, so I'd said you'd ring him. Hope that's ok?" Nikki stared into her mug and tears dropped onto the table.

"Of course I will, yeah. How? How did he die?" she asked.

"Not sure, but he must have been well in his seventies by now, Nik"

"That's not old" she snapped.

"No love, no it *isn't*, I'm so sorry, Nik, I know how much he meant to you." He put his hand on her shoulder. She looked up at him, stood up, hugged him tight and sobbed. Pip just held her, like he always had done when she'd needed him too. After a while, she pulled herself away and wiped her face on her sleeves.

"When's the funeral?" she asked.

"I don't know any more than that yet. Ring Bernis' son. What's his name? I couldn't remember and didn't like to ask".

"Pete. His names Peter" said Nikki. "Yes, yes I'll ring him......."

"Do you want me to stay for a bit." asked Pip.

Nikki stood up and forced a laugh, "Depends what you mean by a bit? she said.

Pip smiled. They both knew that wasn't going to happen. Not today. She was trying to lighten the moment. It didn't though.

"No. But, thank you. Thank you for coming to tell me, I do appreciate it. Suzanne's coming over later. We were going to hit the shops this afternoon but I don't know if I want to now".

Pip didn't want to leave her alone, he could see how upset she was. Nikki showed him to the door and kissed his cheek.

"You go, I'll be alright. Suze will be here, soon." she said.

"If you're sure?" he smiled and went to the van. He opened the door and then turned and walked back to her

"If ever you need *anything*, Nik....." he said tentatively "If you ever need *me*, call me, promise you'll call me, *please*" he sounded so sad. Nikki put her arms round his neck and whispered

"I *will*, I *promise*".

She went back into the house fell onto the sofa and sobbed. It had been nearly two years since she'd seen Danny. They had spoken on the phone often enough, but that's not the same. They sent each other silly jokey gifts, for any and all occasions, Danny had a real skill for finding just the right thing for her albeit a bit risky at times. Tom didn't always approve. This often made the gifts all the more amusing to her. Tom had never understood her relationship with Danny and had refused to have him as Godfather to either of the boys. That had hurt her. Tom said the church didn't approve of gays and Nikki argued that God loved everyone regardless and it shouldn't make any difference. But in the end she had backed down. She thought of all the good times she and Danny had shared together over the years. He had been her best friend and she loved him. How she regretted not making more of an effort to see him. He must have been so lonely. He had never got over losing Berni and once he'd retired from the hotel he saw very few people. He kept himself, his home and his garden immaculate, but that was all he had in his life. Nikki felt dreadful. She should have been there for him, so much more than she was. She hoped he knew what he had meant to her. Nikki cried until her eyes were sore. Every memory of him triggered more tears and regret of not seeing him more. She was grateful that Tom wasn't at home. He wouldn't have understood her grief. She was grateful too that Charley and Harry were out. Charley, especially, found it very hard to see his mother upset. Once she had composed herself, she looked up the number for the *Locomotive* and called Peter. A young woman answered the phone and called through to him. Nikki heard him call back that he'd take the call in the function room. Nikki waited and heard the extension phone pick up.

"Hello Nikki" said Pete, sounding exactly like Berni used too, so much so it took Nikki by surprise.

"Thank you for calling, I'm guessing you've seen Pip?" he asked.

"Yes, this morning, thank you for letting us know, I....." but Nikki couldn't finish her sentence. "Are you ok, sweetheart?" Pete said kindly "I'm sorry, I would have told you myself but I didn't have a number for you. I even looked back in the bookings records but any party you had here was just written in as *my Nikki* in Danny's handwriting."

Nikki smiled. That was sweet.

"When's the funeral Peter?" she asked.

"This coming Friday. Eleven o'clock, at the crematorium. And obviously it's back here afterwards." he replied "Please say you'll be able to come? I've no idea how many to expect...."

"Of course I'll be there" said Nikki.

"There's something else, Nikki, I'm the executor of Danny's will. I made him a promise that I'd make sure everything got sorted out for him. It's what Dad would have wanted too. The thing is, he's left you pretty much everything"

Nikki felt her blood run cold.

"What?" she questioned him "Why?"

"Because he thought the world of you Nikki. You were a true friend to him and my Dad, you never judged them. You brought sunshine into Danny's life, that's what he told me, on more than one occasion. He said he wanted you to be happy and if money was the only thing that prevented that, then maybe he could help. He said you'd know what he meant?"

Nikki started to cry again. Bless him. Danny was the kindest, most thoughtful man she had ever known.

"Thank you, Peter. Is there anything you want me to do?" she asked.

"Well, I wondered if you'd like to say a few words Friday? I know, it's a big ask but...." Before he'd finished his sentence, Nikki interrupted with the fact she would be privileged and of course she would. Peter had arranged to meet up with the vicar on Tuesday to finalize the arrangements and Nikki promised to join them.

"Thanks, I'll see you then" said Nikki

"Don't you want to know exactly what he's left you?" asked Peter. Nikki honestly hadn't thought about it.

"Well, I suppose.... *his house*?" she replied

"Yes Nikki, and his savings. He was very organised and savvy. The funeral was paid for in advance, there are very little costs to settle, so with his insurances and other investments you're looking at somewhere in the region of three quarters of a million."

Nikki felt sick. She didn't know what to say.

"Oh my God, Peter, I had no idea." she stuttered.

"You're a lucky lady." said Peter gently.

"I was........." she replied "Danny was the best friend I ever had."

Chapter Twenty Five

The day of the funeral was really hard. Suzanne and John accompanied Nikki to the small church less than a mile from the *Railway View*. The congregation consisted of a lot of ageing men in garish outfits. Danny had requested bright colours and cerise was apparently the new black. Nikki was pleased to see so many people but she said very little, fighting with herself to hold it together, so she could deliver her epitaph. She spoke well, with fondness and love, for her friend. She made everyone laugh as she recalled some of the escapades they had shared over the years. She balanced a small bell on the lectern, and as she finished speaking, she turned toward the coffin and *pinged* it. "Goodbye Danny" she said and blew a kiss.

It was then the tears streamed from her eyes. She froze, where she stood, and sobbed. She felt a strong arm around her.

Pip led her back to her seat.

"Well done darling" he whispered "Danny would have loved that."

The rest of the day passed slowly. The mood at the

locomotive was sombre. Danny really *wouldn't* have liked that! He'd have been the first to say it was dull and would have probably left.

Nikki smiled to herself, "Cheers Danny." she said quietly, "*I know..... and I would have left with you*". She felt obliged to stay until the last of the attendees had gone. This was only made easier by the support she had had from Pip. He stayed beside her all day. It wasn't until afterwards that she even considered how that may have looked. Not that she cared anymore. But it was surprising that Pip didn't seem to mind either.

It was a few months before the Will was settled and Nikki received a substantial cheque. The cashier behind the counter at the building society looked up at her and used the name Mrs Denton a few too many times enquiring if she had plans for her windfall. Nikki offered no reply, it was none of her business and she was beginning to get annoyed.

"Would you like me to arrange a meeting with our financial advisor, Mrs Denton? With such a large sum of money, I would recommend you speak to him." she said.

"And *I* would recommend, you keep your voice down as I would prefer it if the rest of your customers didn't know my business. No, I do not want to talk to your advisor. I know exactly what I'm going to do with it." Nikki retorted and with that she took her book and left the shop. It was in that moment that she realized she did know *exactly* what she was going to do, but first she really *had* to meet up with Pip. After all, he was going to be the heart of all her plans. She justified her decision on owing Danny that much, at least.

Pip was flirtatious when he answered the phone. Nikki hadn't seen him since the funeral although he *had* rung her, a couple of times to check she was okay. She was pleased he was in a good mood.

"Can you get away for the weekend after next?" she asked thinking he was going to come up with a hundred and one reasons why he couldn't.

"Funny you should ask that, I was going to ask you the same thing." he replied

"*Really*? Bloody hell, Pip, I wish I'd waited now, just for the amazement." she laughed.

"I thought we could rent a cottage in the country, somewhere quiet, just the two of us, what do you think?"

"Perfect, that sounds just perfect, sweetheart" he said. So they made the arrangements.

Tom's job was taking him away more and more these days and it had been Marion who had suggested that Nikki should get a break. She and Derek were looking forward to having Charley and Harry for the weekend. At fifteen and thirteen, both were growing into lovely young men, well mannered and sociable. They were as happy playing cards or board games with their grandparents as they were doing anything else. The only downside to the plans was that Nikki still had to lie. How could she tell her parents who she was going away with? So she didn't. She said she was going to stay with Lyn. Marion barely remembered Nikki's old school friend and hadn't even heard mention of her in the last few years. But she didn't question her. And Nikki didn't offer any more information.

Nikki drove. She picked Pip up close to the railway station. He had told Pat he was going to see Simon. This was easy, Pat would never check up on him and they had rowed about the fact he was going. They had rowed a lot lately and Pip was not at all happy. Pip had an old fashioned sack holdall with him as well as a small case. Nikki looked bemused.

"Some tools for Harry." he smiled, "thought he could make use of them."

"Thanks Pip. That's really thoughtful, he'll be so pleased."

Pip slung the bag onto the back seat. Clunck..

"Well, there goes tonight's supper....." said Nikki

They drove for nearly three hours, chatting singing and laughing. Nikki felt relaxed. The thatched cottage sat in a small clearing at the end of a dirt track. The closest building was a mile and a half away and that was the local shop and post office. Next door to that was a beautiful Tudor built inn. They called in there to collect the cottage key.

After bringing in the bags from the car, Pip lit the fire and Nikki unpacked the few groceries she had brought with them. She smiled at Pip. It was wonderful being here like this with him. They could be apart for months, years at times, but nothing ever changed between them. She loved him. She always had done. She walked over to him and put her arms round his neck. He turned and kissed her gently pushing her down onto the rug in front of the fire. And there they lay for the next few hours making love and barely talking.

Eventually, Pip got up. "I'll open a bottle of wine" he said, "unless you want to go out for something to eat?"

"I just want to stay in with you tonight" said Nikki, "I've got a hotpot already to heat up if that's ok with you, and it's still in once piece since your assault on it earlier".

"Perfect. You're perfect" he said. Nikki had never felt happier.

But what she wanted to talk to him about, would have to wait until tomorrow, just in case.

She didn't want anything to ruin tonight.

After breakfast, they decided to take a leisurely walk before arriving at the pub in time for lunch. Holding his hand, walking together, saying good morning in unison to other walkers and not worrying they might be seen together felt so good. This was all she ever wanted. They looked good together, despite the age gap. They *were* good together.

It was during lunch and after finishing the second pint of real ale, that Nikki plucked up the courage to say her piece. She had rehearsed it enough in her head and could only hope his response would be the one she wanted to hear.

"I been thinking a lot lately, Pip" she started "And I want to ask you something."

"Ooooh, sounds ominous" he said sipping his beer.

"Promise you won't be cross and that you'll let me finish." she went on

"I promise" he smiled.

"I'm leaving Tom. I want to tell Charley and Harry about you and me. It'll make life easier for all of us and I hope that soon, as soon as we are able to, we can be together, live together as a family. The boys adore you, Pip you know they do, they'd love it. They know Tom and I aren't happy. Only last week Charley asked me why we were still married. He thought I needed someone to take me out once in a while. So he and Harry took me to MacDonald's for a treat. Bless them. If they've noticed, Pip, it must be time to move on. And now, thanks to Danny, I believe I can..... we can"

There, she'd said it

. Shit, she'd *blown* it more like. She picked up Pip's beer and glugged down his last quarter pint.

"Ok" said Pip "on one proviso".......

Nikki looked stunned, she hadn't expected this

"What?" she asked

"Stop drinking my bloody beer!" he laughed and went to the bar to get them both a third pint. Nikki wasn't sure she could manage another one. The last two had already gone to her head. Did that just happen? Nikki asked herself, perhaps he hadn't heard her properly. She had just asked him to move in and he said yes. Or had she misunderstood?

Pip put the drinks down on the table and took her hand. He twiddled the small signet ring on her finger. The one he had brought her years before,

"Together, forever...." he said and kissed her passionately. Nikki couldn't believe it. She was so happy, she started to cry.

"I can't win, Nik" joked Pip, "I thought that's what you wanted me to say and now you're crying!"

Nikki wiped her eyes.

"Wow, she said "You never cease to surprise me Mr Scarrow" She picked up her glass

"To us" she said.

"Cheers." replied Pip "Now drink up cos I want to surprise you again."

"Really? How?" she asked.

"By shagging you senseless all afternoon, despite having downed three pints of real ale in less than an hour" they both laughed out loud, Nikki was sure the elderly couple on the next table had heard him. The old man in his flat capped winked at her as she put on her coat. His wife nudged his arm.

Nikki felt she should acknowledge them,

"Bye, enjoy your afternoon" said Nikki as she walked passed them.

"Not as much as you will!" the old man shouted out. Pip roared with laughter as he saw Nikki blush. They left like a couple of silly giggly children and made their way back stopping only for kisses. Pip stood Nikki on his boots and wrapped his jacket around her, walking her backwards as far as he could. They couldn't wait to get back into bed, and Pip was right, he did surprise her.

It was gone seven before either of them awoke. Nikki lay there looking at him. He could sense it and opened one eye.

"What?" he asked

"Just thinking" said Nikki "We've got a hell of a lot to sort out."

"Yes YOU have", smiled Pip

"I'll join in when I know the words. Nothing we can do about it for the next couple of days so let's not get stressed thinking what's got to be done. Please Nik, let's just enjoy this weekend." "Ok, deal." she wasn't going to let anything spoil this. It was after all the beginning of the rest of their lives and this was all she had ever wanted.

Chapter Twenty Six

Tom came home during the day, the following Thursday. Nikki had taken a day off to collect him from the airport. He was moody in the car and she put it down to tiredness. Although he thanked Nikki for picking him up, he always expected her too. He dozed on the way home and Nikki was relieved not to have to make conversation. She did, however, want to talk to him before the boys got in from school. Now she had made the decision, she wanted to get on with it. When they got in, Tom went upstairs for a bath and left Nikki a large bag of his washing to sort out. The return- from –business- trips, were always the same and were one of the things she would miss the least.

He came down stairs in jeans and jumper looking fresh, but surprisingly young and vulnerable, or maybe that's just what Nikki saw as she knew she was about to upset him. She forced herself to start the conversation. It would have been so easy not to have done. She poured him a large red wine and sat in the chair, furthest from him.

"Ssh," he said, "I want to catch the news, one of our

guys is on his way to the Middle East and it's looking very unstable out there." Nikki got up and switched the TV off.

"What you doing? yelled Tom, "I just said I wanted to watch that"

Nikki stood in front of the screen.

"I'm leaving you, Tom. I'm sorry, but we haven't anything in common anymore. I'm unhappy and I've decided it's time for us to part." She looked down at the floor.

"Fine," shouted Tom "now put the telly back on, we can talk about this later."

Nikki walked away from the TV, she picked up a small holdall she had packed up for Tom. She threw it onto the settee next to him.

"Go and watch it at your mothers" she said. "I think we're done here". Tom looked up at her. "I'm not going anywhere, this is my house." he said.

"I know, but for the sake of the boys, you go for now, you can have the house once I've found us somewhere else to live".

"You've got it all worked out haven't you" Tom didn't look hurt or upset, just angry.

"*Please*, Tom, just for tonight at least, I need to talk to the boys."

"What makes you think they will want to stay with you?" he asked.

Nikki laughed

"You're never here, Tom. You couldn't possible give them the stability they need"

This was true but it didn't mean that Tom wasn't going to argue about it. It seemed to Nikki that Tom had been waiting for her to be the first one to suggest they split up.

He didn't put up any real fight to save the marriage. It was inevitable really. They had grown further and further apart. Tom didn't share her interests, he never had and he belittled her job. She had long stopped trying to talk to him about her life and the only conversations they had of any consequence were about the boys and their schooling.

They rowed for nearly an hour over the most petty of things. It was getting close to the time the boys came home from school. Nikki went to fetch them. Tom wouldn't leave the house. She explained to Charley and Harry what had happened and to her surprise neither of them seemed particularly concerned. Charley said he was ok about it as long as he could still see both of them. Harry sarcastically said he let her know if he noticed any difference. Nikki found herself defending Tom. She said that Tom was at home and didn't want to leave, so she would be staying at grandmas' tonight. Tom insisted that the boys stay at home with him that evening and reluctantly Nikki agreed. She went to her parents. She dreaded telling Marion and Derek what had happened. To her surprise, her mother greeted her with "Come in sweetheart, we knew this day would come."

They couldn't have been more supportive. It's funny, when you've rehearsed conversations in your head. You assume you know what other people are going to say. When they don't, it surprises you. Sometimes, just sometimes, things are as bad as you expect them to be.

This was true with Marion and Derek. For a while Derek felt he had somehow failed Nikki, which wasn't true at all. He was a little distant, for a time, but with Marion's support, for both him *and* Nikki, he soon came round to the fact that his little girl was soon to be divorced. He had asked if there was anyone else. Nikki was sure her mother didn't believe her when she said 'no'. It wasn't the right time. Pip wasn't ready. And anyway, she knew that Derek would find it much harder to accept. So for now, at least, it was just going to be her and the boys until they could move on.

Within a few weeks, Tom decided that the time had come to move to London. He had brought a flat there some years earlier as an investment, not that he'd ever told Nikki about it. It was *his* and nothing to do with her. He had worked out of the offices there for years and he had friends there, well good colleagues at least. He promised to visit the boys regularly and they could go and stay with him whenever they liked. Neither he nor Nikki felt anything much when the day came for him to leave. Nikki went back to the family home with Charley and Harry and had agreed with Tom to give him half the market value of the house, which she did. This suited everyone. And within the year, the divorce was absolute.

She planned a few alterations and started to redecorate. Pip was on hand to help, as he always had been, and it was only a couple of weeks after their father had left that Nikki decided to tell the boys about the relationship between her and Pip. The boys seemed genuinely pleased for her and didn't really ask too many questions, which was just as well as there was a lot she didn't want to tell them. They just wanted their mum to be happy. They had always liked Pip and easily accepted him into their home. Bit by bit Pip brought more and more of his work tools round for Harry. Nikki felt at last he was beginning to show real commitment.

For now, at least, Marion and Derek weren't to know.

After all, Pip was still married. Nikki planned a week away for her, Pip and the boys, in the autumn half -term. This would be an ideal time, Nikki thought, to nudge Pip into taking the final step.

The holiday was wonderful. The boys were relaxed with Pip, and it seemed the most natural thing that they should all be together. Pip took Nikki's hand as they strolled along the beach in the cool evening air. This was just perfect.

"This is all I've ever wanted Pip." she said as she snuggled her head into his chest.

"Me too, sweetheart" he said. The time is right, thought Nikki. I'll ask him to move his stuff in when we get back. She did. This was another of those conversations she had in her head that didn't go as planned.

"I can't, Nik, not yet."

"Why, Pip? What's stopping you *now*? You know what we'd planned" she said.

"It's easy for you, Nik. It's too complicated for me right now." he replied.

"*Easy*?" said Nik, raising her voice slightly, "How the hell is being a single parent, going through a divorce and constantly having to lie to my parents, easy?"

Pip let go of her hand and put his hands in his pockets.

"It's mum" he said. "She's not at all well at the moment. It would break her heart if Pat and I split up. I can't do it to her Nik, it would finish her" Nikki knew how much his mum meant to him. She was the reason Pip had carried the can for Simon all those years ago. Nikki had never really understood that, but she had accepted it. Now however, she was going to have to wait for Pip again. This didn't seem fair but she'd waited this long.

"You haven't changed your mind, Pip, have you?" she asked after a long pause.

"No, no, of course not. Just don't rush me Nik. In the mean time we can still be together, much more often now the boys know. We'll *get* there darling. Just not right now" He wrapped his strong arms round her and she felt small. He always took charge and she would melt into him and let him. Having him like this was better than not at all. That was going to have to be enough for now.

"Just for the record, Pip, I don't think we can be accused of rushing anything, it's twenty one years since you first kissed me."

"Really? Bloody hell, is it? Still, the best things in life are worth waiting for." Pip laughed.

Nikki smiled.

"If you say so" she said.

"Oooh, do I detect little Miss Grumpy?" Pip said teasing her.

"No, not really, but you can detect little Miss *'I've learnt to stick up for myself'* if you like."

Pip laughed at her. But Nikki went on.

"I'll wait a bit longer Pip. But not *forever*. If this is all you're offering I need to know now. If you haven't moved in by the time your sixty five, that's it. I want some of the good years with you, not just the *final* years. Sorry, if that sounds harsh, but I think it's reasonable. So sort yourself out, you've just over five years".

"Fair enough," grinned Pip, "I love it when you're assertive, can we go back to the apartment now. The boys are out." He hugged her so tight she could hardly breathe and she had to struggle to get loose. He made her laugh, but she had meant what she said.

And so, that's how it went on, for the next three or four years. Pip visited regularly, stayed over at the house about one weekend in every four or five. He ate meals with them, holidayed occasionally and never spent Christmas with them. Nikki had found herself settling for this life. She was, after all, the other woman, although this wasn't how she saw herself.

Charley had left for university and was working towards a degree in journalism. Harry had left school at sixteen and had completed a course for carpentry. Pip had helped him no end with this and encouraged him to go on to do a full apprenticeship. He took his driving test, got himself a van and had set himself up as a general handyman. The wealth of experience both Derek and Pip were able to offer proved invaluable and Harry soon made a success of himself. With both the boys now much more independent, Nikki wanted Pip around more.

It was after the two of them had finished dinner one evening she broached the subject of him moving in again. Pip put down his cutlery.

"I can't, Nik, not just now. Mums taken a turn for the worse." he said. Nikki couldn't help but smile.

"Really, Pip?" she replied "I thought that was your excuse last time."

Pip got up and put the plates in the sink. He started to run the tap.

"We need to talk, Nik, but let's get the washing up out of the way first" They finished the dishes and took the rest of the wine bottle into the living room.

"Something's happened, Nik. Carries' daughter Chloe, you remember me telling you she'd been poorly? Well she needed a kidney transplant."

Nikki looked at Pip. Yes he had mentioned Chloe before, but they rarely talked about Carrie or her kids, Nikki wasn't that interested. Carrie was a selfish bitch and Nikki had always felt annoyed by her - even though they had never met. Carrie had always been yet another obstacle that prevented Pip and her being together. Or at least that was how it seemed. So what had any of this got to do with them now?

"Well," Pip continued, "Simon went to see if he was a match for her. He thought it his duty. He hoped it could make amends, in some way".

Then came the bombshell.

"Anyway, it turns out that Simon wasn't only *not* a match for Chloe, he wasn't even her DNA." Pip drank his wine and looked at the floor. Nikki glared at him.

"Do you mean he's *not* Carrie father after all? Bloody hell, Pip. .... oh my God. She's not yours is she?" she asked

"Of *course* not! I told you what had happened. I was never part of that!" Pip looked cross, but he went on, "Simon and I confronted Pat last week and she admitted that she was pregnant *before* the rape happened. Simon had always denied she was raped at all. By any of them. Pat had a bit of a reputation in those days. She had drinking with them on the night it happened and was up-for-it as much as anyone. It was only the next morning she decided to say she was attacked. The police believed her story and wouldn't listen to Si. She wanted him to pay. Well, she wanted someone to pay. Turns out, we both did........God, she's one scheming bitch. It's all been one big fucking lie. To think I felt sorry for her all these years. I thought I was doing the right thing. And I still can't get out of it."

Pip was angry and upset. Nikki held him tight.

"It's ok, Pip. You're ok, I'm here for you. You know I am. I *always* am" She left it a few minutes before asking why he couldn't get out of it.

"Pat's threatened to tell mum about the rape charge, and we can't prove it isn't true. Mum would realize we've lied to her all this time. It would break her heart to know Simon's been in prison. She's too frail. It'll finish her. I can't let that happen."

Nikki just held him and then he repeated.

"Pat's going to tell mum Nik, I can't let that happen."

"I know" said Nikki, "You just said that."

"What?" questioned Pip "I just said what?"

"You just said Pat's going to tell your mum."

"Tell her what?" said Pip" he looked so confused and Nikki started to get worried.

"Pip, you just said Pat going to tell your mum about the rape and you couldn't let that happen. Don't you remember saying that?" Nikki asked.

Pip shrugged.

"Well, I can't let it happen." he said. He got up and took the wine glasses into the kitchen. Nikki followed him through.

Pip stood by the sink. He was running the cold tap into the empty wine glass and wiping a j-cloth round and round the rim. Nikki turned the tap off.

"Are you ok, darling" she asked putting her arms round his waist.

228

"Yeah. I'm okay, just been getting a bit forgetful lately. Stress I 'spose. It's been a bloody awful couple of weeks. I'll be alright. Don't worry." he kissed her forehead.

"I'm going to have to go, I'm afraid. Sorry, darling. I've got a lot to sort out."

They went to small hallway and Pip put his jacket on.

"Thank you." he smiled

"What for?"

"For being you. My Nikki. I love you, you do know that don't you?" he said as he tenderly kissed her goodnight.

"You haven't said that for a while" she smiled "I love you too, always."

After he had left, Nikki thought about the conversation they had had. She was worried about him. He had forgotten quite a lot of things lately. People's names, places, appointments, that sort of thing, but Pip had always laughed it off, like he had always done with so many things. He put it down to old age and referred to himself as a 'dopey ol' bugger'. But Nikki was worried. She feared it was maybe more than that.

The arguments in Pips house, over the next week or so, were aggressive and scary. Pat was violent and Pip had walked out on a number of occasions. This had only added to Pats anger.

The truth had, at last come out about the lie Pat had forced them all to live, for all those years. She had lived with the pretence for so long, that she believed it all to be true. And she showed no remorse to either Pip or Simon. Pip was doing all he could to protect his mother.

It was during a particularly loud argument that Simon

arrived at the house. Pat screamed at Pip to make him leave. Pip stepped outside to see him.

"She's lost it Si," said Pip, "I can't take much more of this"

Simon looked at his brother,

"You won't have to, mate. None of us will. I'm sorry, Pip......." said Simon. Pip looked at him.

"No. Oh no, Si. She's gone hasn't she?" He could feel the tears well in his eyes.

"Yes," said Simon, "The home called me about half an hour ago, I said we were on our way." "Let's just go." said Pip and went to get into Simons car.

"You might want to put some shoes on, mate."

Pip looked at his socks. "Yeah, yeah give me a minute."

Pip got into the car.

"How is she?" he asked.

"How's who?"

"Mum. How is she? repeated Pip.

Simon frowned at him

"She's *dead*, Pip. That's how she is!"

Pip sank back into his seat. Neither brother spoke for the rest of the journey to the nursing home.

Chapter Twenty Seven

After the funeral, Simon invited Pip to stay with him for a while. Pip was grateful for the offer. The arrangements had taken their toll on Pip. He had been devoted to his mother and her death had hit him hard. Simon and Pip had grown closer again over the past couple of years. Pip, was a forgiving man and, despite everything there had gone through, he loved his brother. He was glad to get away from Pat for a while too. But he missed Nikki.

One evening, Simon had taken Pip out for a pub supper. It was spring time and the two men sat outside watching the rowing eights practicing for the May bumps.

"Are you *still* going to stay with her now?" asked Simon as he put the beers down.

"Yes of course, we'll always be together. We made that promise years ago. Together, forever." Pip smiled into his beer. Simon stared at him.

"Are you for real? After the hell she's put you though?"
Pip grinned.

"She's never put me through hell," he laughed, "Bit

demanding at times, if you get my drift, but no way would you call that hell."

Simon looked confused.

"Who are we are talking about?"

"Nikki. My, Nikki" said Pip, "Who would I be talking about?"

"Well I was talking about Pat. Who the hell's Nikki?" asked Simon.

Pip looked like a rabbit in headlights.

"Nikki? Why do you ask?"

"Cos you're talking about her Pip. What's the matter with you?"

Pip drank his beer.

"I don't know, Si. I can't think straight anymore, I get muddled, I say stuff I shouldn't. I forget things. I'm worried. I don't think I'm very well".

"How long has it been going on?" asked Simon

"About six or seven months, I 'spose. I just thought it was my age but I'm not so sure now." Pip looked serious. "It's getting worse. I'll make myself an appointment at the doc's when I get back"

"Make sure you do" replied Simon "But I meant how longs it been going on with this Nikki?" Simon winked at him. The smile returned to Pip face and his blue eyes twinkled.

"Oh, not that long," he said and took another sip of beer before adding "about twenty five years!"

Simon lifted his glass, "Good for you, son! Do I get to meet her?"

"I hope so." smiled Pip.

It was three weeks before Pip returned home. The two

brothers had spent the time sorting out their mothers' things and making sure any loose ends were tied up. Pip had needed this time to morn. He also needed time to decide what he was going to do next. Simon had assured him of his help in finally leaving Pat and helping him to start the life with Nikki he had always wanted.

"We need to start making some serious plans mate," Simon told his brother, "and we must make sure Pat knows nothing about Nikki. If she finds out, she'll take you for every penny. We need to protect you and your assets. That includes your little Nikki!" he said with a wink. "Have you made a Will?"

"No, not yet, but I need to. I have thought about it a lot, I know what I want to do." replied Pip. Simon took out his phone and took charge.

"I'll call my solicitor. We can get this sorted"

The next morning, Simon took Pip to make his Will. He had thought long and hard as to how he could do the best he could for Nikki. If he was to go before her, he wanted her to have what was his. This was actually very little now. As it stood, Pat would be entitled to half the house, but that was it. As far as he was concerned he owed her nothing else. Truth was, he didn't have much else. His business had been winding down over the past few months and he planned to pass on anything of benefit, to Harry. He was, after all, like the son he never had. Pip had seen a lot of his younger self in him. Pip had re- mortgaged his house to support Carrie some ten years ago and consequently there was now probably more debt than equity. There was some jewellery that belonged to his mother and he wanted Nikki to have that. She would treasure it – he knew that.

Simon had also promised to accompany Pip to see the doctor the following week as whatever it was that was making Pip confused was getting worse. So much so, that by the time he returned home, he couldn't remember where he lived. To the relief of both of them, Pat was out.

It was Simon who rang Nikki to say they were home. Pip's number came up on her phone "Hello, darling," she answered "Are you back safe?"

Simon interrupted her before she said anything else.

"It's Simon, Pip's brother. Hello Nikki."

"Oh. Err. Hi. How are you?" she stuttered.

Well, this *was* a first, Pip had actually told someone else about them. She felt surprised and really happy. This was a big step forward.

"I'm fine, thank you, Pip's told me *all* about you."

Nikki hoped he hadn't told him too much, but was secretly pleased. Then she felt a rush of panic. Why was Simon ringing and not Pip?

"Is he ok?"

"Yes. Well sort of. Have you noticed him getting confused lately?" he asked.

Nikki and Simon spoke for a while about their concerns for Pip's condition. He assured her he would make sure he saw the doctor the following day.

"Where is he now?" she asked.

"Just coming out the house, I'll put him on."

"Who are you talking to? Pip asked Simon as he took his phone.

"Hello?" said Pip "Who's this?"

"It's me, Nikki, Hello darling, how are you?"

"How did you get Si's number?" Pip asked.

Nikki laughed

"I didn't, he rang me on your phone. He thinks it's about time we got introduced, I do too. Come and have your dinner tonight before Simon goes back, both of you. Charley and Harry are home. He might as well get to meet us all. The boys haven't seen you in ages, Pip, say you'll come"

Pip smiled,

"See you at seven." he said "Love you."

Nikki was unusually nervous getting the meal ready. She was looking forward to meeting Simon. For years she had pictured him as an angry dangerous criminal, but now she saw him as Pips brother, someone else who was looking out for the man she loved and that was all that mattered to her. Harry couldn't wait to meet someone who had actually *done time inside* as he so eloquently put it, but Nikki had asked him not to pry or make Simon feel uncomfortable. She really needn't have worried. Simon chatted with the boys like a long lost uncle and they all got on fine. Nikki liked Simon. He was very like Pip in a lot of ways, but much heavier, shorter and much more common in the way he spoke. Other than that, they had a similar sense of humour and the same flirtatious behaviour! It was all in good humour though and Nikki found herself loving the attention from both men as they fought playfully for her attention. Charley told Simon he was wasting his time as his mum had only every loved Pip - all her life- and no one else came close. Pip grinned from ear to ear.

This was true but Nikki felt a twinge of sadness that Charley thought she had never loved his father. But she said nothing and just squeezed Charley's hand. Harry was deep in conversation with Simon about '*lifers*' when Nikki returned to the table with the dessert. She had made a lemon sponge and custard. It was Pip and Harrys' favourite. They always argued over who would get the last piece or the extra lemon that had run down the sides of the bowl.

"Baggsi I get the serving plate, Pip" said Harry. Pip looked over to him,

"Yes of course, I don't like lemon." he said.

"Sure you do, you *always* fight me for it" said Harry.

"I've *never* liked Lemon, John, you've known that since college." snapped Pip.

"What the fuck?" laughed Harry.

"Harry!" snapped Nikki "I *won't* have that language like that at the table."

"Well, who's John?" asked Harry.

"I think it's, Uncle John. Pip went to college with him." said Nikki kindly.

"Well that ain't me is it? And he does like lemon" Harry went on.

"Just *leave* it, Harry *please*" said Nikki. Pip stared at the plate in front of him and ate the sponge and custard. Charley gave Harry a look that told him to shut up. No one said a word until they had all finished.

Simon drove Pip home and promised to call Nikki after they had seen the doctor in the morning.

Nikki's phone rang about noon. Simon was at the hospital with Pip who was having a C.T scan.

"The GP sent us straight here. Try not to worry, Nik," said Simon kindly. But she could hear in his voice that *he* was worried.

"When will we know the results?" she asked.

"I'm not sure, noone's telling me much, I promise you'll know as soon as I do." he went on. Then Nikki heard Pat in the background, she was there with them.

"I'm sorry love, I've got to go, talk later." and with that Simon hung up. Nikki felt alone and fearful for Pip. Times like this were so hard. *She* should be with him. Not Pat.

It was late that evening when Simon rang her back. He explained that the scan had shown a large growth on Pips brain and the surgeons were going to operate in the morning.

Chapter Twenty Eight

The next few weeks were really horrible - for everyone. Pip had a second operation but the surgeons had told Pat and Simon that there wasn't very much more they could do to help. The tumour, although now reduced in size, was aggressive and they could do little more than monitor Pip and try to keep his pain under control for what was to be quite likely, a slow deterioration. Pip was as positive as he could be despite not being able to work. For now, at any rate, he was still able to lead a relatively normal life despite having to surrender his driving licence. It was also advised that he wasn't to be left on his own for too long. Nikki was so grateful that Simon was back in his life and that Pip had told him about her before this all happened. It meant Simon would bring Pip round for the day, while Pat was at work and leave them alone before collecting him to take him back in the evening. Nikki felt wanted. He was after all, still her man and he really needed her now. They sat for hours, just holding hands, talking or laying in bed together, side by side just holding each other. These days were so precious and Nikki knew it. But as the weeks passed, it got harder and harder for her to let him leave.

Pip had spent a lovely day with Nikki. It had now been six weeks since his surgery and his deterioration was really noticeable, not just with his speech and his appetite but the sparkle, the one that made Pip, Pip, was much dimmer. Simon came to pick him up and took Pip back to the house he still shared with Pat. Pip was tired and wanted to get to bed. But Pat insisted the three of them talked together. Since Pip had stopped work, money was getting tight. Pat was fully aware that the care Pip needed may well turn out to wipe them out completely. She wasn't going to let that happen. Half of what they had belonged to her, and she was going to make sure she got it. Pat was going to have to get things moving quickly as Pip was already beginning to need more help. She wasn't prepared to give that either, why should she? They had done nothing but argue for years and she felt very little, if anything, for him.

"I've arrange for you to go into the nursing home for a couple of weeks," she said coldly, You're to have an assessment to see what help we need and anyway, I need a break." She took a mouthful of red wine from her glass.

"No," said Pip, "I d-d-d-don't need that, not yet, I'm not g-going"

"It's all *arranged*." replied Pat, "The doctor thinks it's best to have everything ready for when you do. It won't be long before you need full time care. I can't do that Philip, you can't expect me to" The way she spoke to him was heartless. Simon was furious but Pip didn't have the fight to argue.

"Whatever." said Pip, "I suppose the rest will do me good."

"Good, I knew you'd see sense, we can go anytime after ten tomorrow morning."

Simon followed her through to the kitchen.

"Why are you doing this? You know it's only a matter of time before he has to go for good, can't you at least try and make him feel wanted at home for a little while longer?"

Simon was crafty. He knew what he was doing. He wanted it to be Pat who made the decisions. He wanted to force her hand, but he wanted his brother to be happy, as much as he could be, in the time he had left. He wanted Pip to be free to spend the rest of his life with Nikki, the woman he could clearly see, totally adored him. The woman he knew would look after him.

"If you're not going to look after him, Pat," he continued, "let him go and get on with your own life. But don't drag it out and make him any more miserable than he already is."

Simon said and he went back to the living room.

Pat thought about what he'd said and planned what she was going to say. She refilled her wine glass and finished the rest of the wine by drinking directly from the bottle.

She walked purposefully back to join the two men. She stood in the doorway, leaning on the architrave.

"I know you've wanted rid of me for years," she said "So, I'll make it easy for you, I want a divorce" she said coldly.

"You *bitch*" said Simon, "Why now? No, let me guess, you want half the house before it gets spent on Pips care?"

"Something like that. It's no more than I deserve." she replied.

Pip sat quietly on the settee. He looked up at Simon.

"No more arguments, Simon", he said softly "Let's get

this sorted out, while I still can. I owe her that." he said and looked intently at his brother.

Both men knew he meant he owed it to *Nikki*, but that wasn't how Pat took it.

"Good," she said, "at least we all agree on something."

There was a brief pause as Pat finished off the wine.

"You can leave now." said Pip and Simon went to stand up, but Pip grabbed his arm.

"Not you, Si. You, P-P-Pat. You leave, leave now. My solicitor will be in t-t-touch."

"What? Oh, no. I'm not going anywhere. I haven't got anywhere to go?" she said

"Not *my* problem anymore. Just go."

Simon stood up and took Pat's elbow,

"You've got five minutes." he said sternly, "Pack a bag. I'll give you a lift."

He drove Pat to the *Railway View* Hotel.

"I've heard the rooms here are very good." he said as he dropped her bag on the pavement and drove away.

The two men talked for a while and decided they would tell Nikki what had happened after they had taken a look at the nursing home. He might as well keep the appointment, he would have to go and visit sometime anyway.

The home was nice, clean and welcoming. Pip introduced himself and tied to explain that he wasn't ready to come in, not just yet. But today wasn't a good day for him and his speech was slurred and he felt unsteady on his feet. Simon could see his frustration and took charge.

"Good morning" smiled the receptionist "How may I help you?"

"Yes, good morning," replied Simon "Mr Scarrow, Philip Scarrow, I think you're expecting us?"

"Ah yes, we have you booked in for the next two weeks. I'll just call someone to show you to your room."

"Change of plan, love. We just wanted to have a look today, I don't think my bruvver is ready for all this yet. I'm sorry to mess you about" he told the young lady. Her expression changed

"There is high demand for places here Mr Scarrow. If you wish for your brother to be removed from the waiting list please say so now. There are many more patients waiting to take his place" she said sternly.

"No love. Don't do that, just not just yet, ok?" Simon said as he turned round to see Pip making his way to the door. Pip had already seen enough. This place was full of old people. He wasn't old, he was sixty- four. He should of had years left in him yet. He walked outside and leant against the white stone wall. Simon followed just a few minutes later.

"Come on, mate," he said cheerfully, "Let's go and see that lovely lady of yours."

This was the first time today Pip had smiled.

Nikki opened the door.

"He's got something he wants to tell you, Nikki," smiled Simon "and about bloody time too, if you ask me. I'm off, call me if you need to. Otherwise see you tomorrow."

Nikki waved goodbye and shut the door.

"Can you stay tonight?" she asked Pip "Where does Pat think you are?"

Pip grinned. "Sh,ssh heee wants a d-d-d-divorce." he said.

Nikki felt her heart miss a beat.

"Really?" she couldn't believe it. "So can we be together now, Pip?" she said and stared into his eyes.

"If y-y-y-you s-s-s- still want me?"

Nikki couldn't hold back her tears any longer.

"Yes, darling. Oh yes. You know I do" she sobbed as she held him tight and he cried into her chest as if he was a small child.

They spent the day quietly together. Nikki read some of the evening paper to him. She served homemade chicken and mushroom soup for their supper. Pip wasn't very hungry and everything he did was becoming more and more of an effort. Nikki looked over at Pip. He was staring at the T.V and not really following the episode of *Morse* that was on. He looked so tired. She was determined she would do whatever it took now, to make him happy. As happy as he could be, anyway. Thanks to the money Danny had left her, she didn't need to work and would be able to care for him, full time. If that's what was needed. She loved him, totally and was prepared to do anything for him.

It was a little after nine o'clock when he said he was ready for bed. Nikki joked with him that it would take more that a brain tumour to stop him getting her into bed at the first available opportunity, and he managed to laugh with her as they went up the stairs.

"I'll ring the boys in the morning." she told him "They'll be so pleased you're here. I expect they'll be over in a day or two to see you."

Pip smiled "I'd like that."

Nikki helped Pip into bed and then got undressed herself. They lay side-by-side, warm and contented.

"I m-m-m-made it" said Pip,

"Made what?" asked Nikki

"I moo, moooved in b- b-b-before I'm s-sixty five."

Nikki laughed

"Cut it a bit fine, didn't you? You've only got two days to spare! Shall we do a bit of a tea party on Saturday?"

Pip nodded "Only...... if you a-ask your D-D-Derek and Marion. It's t-t-time t-to be honest, s-s-s-sweetheart."

"Thank you, Pip" sighed Nikki "I've hated lying to my parents all these years. It's all going to be okay isn't it? We're together now."

Nikki lay back on the pillow with her arm cradling Pips head. He was soon asleep and dribbling on her nightdress.

She lay there thinking of all the good times they had shared and now, at last, she had him all to herself. She would love and look after him. Whatever it took. It was all she had ever wanted to do. There was no way she was going to let him go, not now, not after waiting all these years.

It wasn't long before she too fell asleep.

She woke with a start about three A.M. Pip was staring up at the ceiling. She could see his eyes reflecting the moonlight. The same, beautiful twinkling blue eyes, that had hidden so much over the years.

"Are you okay, darling?" she asked.

Pip lay quiet and said nothing.

"Pip?" she said, she had panic and fear in her voice

"Pip?" she repeated.

Pip blinked, he forced a smile.

"It's alright, Pip, I'm here" she said softly.

Pip squeezed her hand.

"Together... forever" he whispered, before closing his eyes for the very last time.

About the Author

I was born in Cambridge, England in the early 1960's and am the youngest of four siblings. I have three grown up sons of which I am extremely proud. I enjoy gardening, music, walks on the beach, cooking, swimming and more recently writing. I would like to thank my family and dearest friends for all the love and support they give me, after all it is they who make me the person I am.